ALONE
TOGETHER

Sarah J. Donovan

Text copyright © 2018 by Sarah J. Donovan
Photographs copyright © 2018 by Jean Clough
Jacket design and art by April Dippy
Edited by Josiah Davis
Design by Eight Little Pages

ISBN 978-0-9998768-0-0 (hardback) | ISBN 978-0-9998768-3-1 (paperback)
ISBN 978-0-9998768-6-2 (ebook) | ASIN B07BDPXMWH (audiobook)

Printed in the United States of America
10 9 8 7 6 5 4 3 2 1

Seela Books supports the First Amendment and celebrates the right to read.

For Number Ten

AUGUST

SEPTEMBER

OCTOBER

NOVEMBER

DECEMBER

JANUARY

FEBRUARY

MARCH

APRIL

MAY

JUNE

AUGUST

ARRESTED

I knew he'd come,
he'd be the one
because Mom's always at church
these days,
because he's always in the garage
these days.

I knew he'd be stoic
as he shook the hand
of the police commander—
a 6' 6" Santa Claus
with a badge.

Nobody speaks
for what feels like
forever.

I say a silent prayer—
for *what* I don't know.
God has more important
things to worry about
these days.

Dad leans back in his chair.
Crosses his legs.
I notice his overgrown toenails
stretching just beyond the sole
of his too-small flip flops.
Laces his hands behind his head.
I notice the stench of several shower-free days
seeping into the silence.

Santa runs his hands through his silver hair,
smoothes out his beard,
blue eyes taking note of this
father-daughter dynamic.

"Today's my last day," says Santa.
"and it looks to me
like you could use
a break."

I'm not sure
if he's talking to me,
if he's talking to Dad,
but my hands are praying
for some miracle.

Santa
tosses my violation in the trash.
Santa
stands to shake my hand.

My fingers are lost in his palm, and
I swear his blue eyes twinkle as he says,
"Make better choices, Sadie."

Christmas in August, I think.
A Christmas miracle, I think.

Until Dad finally breaks his silence to say,
"Got a few bucks for gas?"

I'm not sure
if he's talking to me,
if he's talking to Santa,
but Santa takes out a ten
and hands it to Dad.

SISTER SADIE

The only one of eleven

who sets the table every morning
with cereal bowls and spoons,

who matches mounds of socks
without complaint or disdain,

who obeys every stand, kneel, sing in mass
without sneaking out after communion.

The only one
who follows the rules,
who keeps the peace,
who has a chance at
joining the convent
to make her old Italian grandmother
proud.

Now
without proper punishment,
without penance or consequence,
without a way to assuage the conscience:

Destined-to-Go-to-Hell Sadie
(or at least confession),
which is okay because
I like boys too much to
become
a
nun.

SILENCE IN NUMBERS

No one is home.
No one.

#1 left at 18 to raise her own family—
    done being a second mother to the brood.
#2 left at 18 to train for triathlons—
    practically ran to Arizona the day he graduated.
#3 was kicked out at 18—
    an unforgivable sin, but we don't talk about her.

I don't know them all that well.
They never come home.

#4 and #5 left to go to college—
    have jobs on campus in the cafeteria,
    wish I could see those boys washing dishes.
#6 left at 18 for restaurant management training—
    didn't have the smarts for college,
    wish I could see her running a crew.

I don't know them all that well.
They never come home.

#7 runs a drive-thru
    passing the time with college classes
    until her boyfriend proposes.
#8 bakes croissants
    saving every bit of dough
    until she can plan her escape.

#10 runs with a gang
    taking #11 to babysitting gigs
    until she sneaks out to party.

I don't know them all that well.
I was busy shoplifting.

ALWAYS HOME

Dad does not have a job.
Fired five years ago,
he
delivered packages
until he didn't,
remodeled a neighbor's basement,
which is still not finished,
designed a truck
that already exists.

So he is making a wooden canoe
in the garage
to one day drift on rivers of bliss,
only
while he's been at "work,"
one through six have already departed,
and seven through eleven
are
making
plans
to
abandon
ship
(or canoe).

SPACE

When I was just two,
we'd outgrown our
Chicago apartment.
Dad gave up teaching
for a good,
corporate job
editing a magazine.

We moved to Lilac Lane:
three bedrooms,
two-car garage,
basement,
patio with porch.
Our palace in the `burbs.

Dad had a plan—
drywall to divide the master
in two,
plywood and paneling to divide the basement
in three.
Seven bedrooms and privacy.

The oldest ones would get private spaces in the basement.
The youngest ones would share the rooms upstairs.

As a sophomore,
with the oldest ones gone,
I gained access to a private chamber
in the basement
of our palace.

Six feet by eight feet
of concrete and paneling,
a wooden door
that locks with a latch,
a 4-inch foam bed.
My precious space.

STEALING POP-TARTS

You know how Pop-Tarts
have six in a box?
Well, six of anything
was never enough
in our house.

When I heard the garage door open
and the Sportabout roll in
to the non-workshop side
of the garage,
I'd turn off the TV
and race to help Mom
unload the boxes and bags
of groceries from Aldi.

Sister Sadie
is a good helper.

I'd always offer to put away
the boxes:
cereal,
Hamburger Helper, and
Pop-Tarts.

When I saw Mom's back turned
and the coast of siblings was clear,
I'd remove a package of two tarts
and hide it behind the
canned carrots, which nobody ever ate.

And in the middle of the night,
when the last of my siblings
slumbered on floors,
I'd hide in the bathroom
and enjoy my Pop-Tarts in peace.
No one ever suspected
Sister Sadie.

THOU SHALT NOT STEAL

I didn't plan to steal the dress.
I didn't plan for Whispers of Want
to take over my soul.
I didn't plan to sin.
Thou shalt not steal
anything but Pop-Tarts.

I was in the stockroom
unpacking a delivery,
steaming out the wrinkles,
price-tagging the garments.

My mind drifted to friends:
Natalie's Chuck Taylors in pink,
Nelly's True Religions frayed in the knees.

My eyes drifted to me:
#8's hand-me-down, white-shoe-polished Keds, one size too big,
#5's *borrowed* 32x36 Levi's, because only his jeans are long
enough,
#6's *borrowed* tank that I wore under a hoodie to hide from her.
(So I guess I'd been "borrowing" clothes since puberty.)

And then I started doing the math:
$80 for tall jeans
+$20 for an infinity scarf
+$100 for a jean jacket
-10 percent employee discount
=

no money for school books, gas for work,
no contacts to see and not look nerdy,
no tampons, have to use Mom's maxi-pads stash.

And then, the Whispers of Want
took over my soul:
You deserve something nice all your own.
You see, it's made for your five-eleven frame.
You'll look gorgeous for Dean at homecoming.
You deserve something pretty, and don't you just
want it? Yes. Yes. Yes.

There I was staring at myself in this
cream, knee-length, tank dress,
sequins draped across my growing chest,
fabric flat along my strong stomach,
A-line drape from the hips—
not-too-tight.
I was beautiful.
And, yes, I wanted that $200 dress.
So, I pulled on my brother's jeans
bunched up the dress around my waist
and zipped up my hoodie
in a moment of utter weakness.

Thou shalt not covet dresses
you cannot afford.

But I knew that.

CAUGHT

The next day,
Dad dropped me off at work.
I paid him gas money to get home.
I went into the store,
and just as I was about to
clock in.

"Sadie, can you come into the office,"
said my manager.
"This is our loss prevention expert,
Mr. Nelson. He is here today to interview
all
employees."

"I just have a few questions.
This won't take long."

Oh. My. God.
My conscience began to scream.
Confess. Confess. You must confess.

"As you know, we have security cameras
throughout the store to prevent loss from shoppers,
but we also have cameras in the stockroom
to prevent loss from
employees."

"Mr. Nelson, you don't have to say another word.
I did it.
I confess.
I stole a dress."

And when Mr. Nelson excused himself
to talk to my manager,
Joelle, a coworker, snuck her head in:
"Whatever you do, don't confess to anything.
He'll say there are cameras, but he's bluffing.
We unplugged them months ago.
It's just a tactic to trap us.
Our discount sucks. "

"Thanks, Joelle," I said.

CONTRITION

I step into the dark, wooden
confessional.
It is oddly like my bedroom
except
there is a kneeler.

Lowering my body
before a symbol of God,
below a man with the power
who slides a window open
to absolve
deeds,
to assuage
shame—
humbling,
humiliating.

"Bless me, Father,
for I have sinned.
It has been,
well,
one day
since my last
confession.

"I am a thief.
I cannot silence
the Whispers of Want.
I want a real bed.
I want my own clothes.
I want a car like my friends.
I want my dad to get a job.
I want my mom to take me shopping.
I want my parents to pay for school.
Heck, I want to toast my Pop-Tarts
and eat them for breakfast!"

"Okay, okay, my child.
Your penance is this:
pray four Hail Marys."

"What? That's it?
What about the Whispers of Want?
How do I make them go away?
I can't be coming back here every day
to
confess."

"Just pray."

I thought I was praying.
I'm kneeling for heaven's sake.

FINDING A NEW JOB

Dad doesn't tell anyone
about my sin
except to say,
"Sadie needs a new job.
School fines are due.
We'll be asking for rent soon."

Mom offers to take me
to clean banks at 4 a.m.,
which I did in elementary school.
No, thanks.

#8, Faith, says the bakery needs
a dishwasher on weekends,
with a look on her face that hints,
I don't want you to work with me.

#7, Hannah, says I should
be a server at Luigi's.
Walking distance. Tips.
He'll even take your work permit.
Plus, she says,
you're just so good at taking orders.

She had me at
"walking distance."

Asking
for anything
from anyone
in this family
is like
squeezing blood
from a stone.

PREP WORK

In the walk-in cooler
I close the door—
a moment alone
to catch my breath,
to stop sweating
from my mile-long walk
in 90 degree August heat,
to gather lettuce heads
in a large black tub
for the antipasti salad.

"Need some help?
You've been in there awhile,"
he says peeking into the cooler.

"No, thanks," I say.

Geesh, can't I have
even a moment of privacy?

I bang eleven heads on the
stainless steel sink,
pop out the cores,
peel off the wilted layers,
wash away the dirt and grime,
and gently tear the leaves
into bite-size pieces.

"Need some help with that?" he calls.

"No, thanks," I say.

And then I see his hands
take the tub from mine.

"I can carry that, you know?" I shout.

"I know," he calls walking away.

I can't help admiring his man-bun
as I dry my hands
on my apron for the
Sunday lunch shift.

Prep work
done.

FAMILY MEETING, PART 1

Mom stands over the kitchen sink—
her bracelets
clank against the stainless steel,
making music with the glasses and plates
as she hums a church tune.

We typically eat all our meals on our own:
peanut butter and grape jelly sandwiches,
cereal,
generic mac and cheese if a few of us are home,
hot dogs and canned lima beans if Dad's around.

Family meetings begin with a mandatory meal.
A mandatory meal means
every inch of the picnic benches filled,
bottoms-by-bottoms,
elbows out just enough to eat
the boxed beef stroganoff Mom prepares.

We eat quickly to get to the part when
we find out why we are here
together.

I think I know.

Mom never joins us at the table.
I wonder if she does not want to eat with us.
I wonder if she prefers her elbow room at the sink.
I wonder if she is imagining a bigger table.
I wonder if she is imagining a different life.

Mom, you can have my seat.
I want to stand at the kitchen sink
alone
to imagine
and have a little more elbow room.

FAMILY MEETING, PART 2

Children sit on the stairs
like a choir on risers
waiting for their director
to blow the pitch pipe.

Dad
stands before the choir,
calls over his wife to sit.
She refuses,
pretending to dry dishes.
Clears his throat
in a guttural cough
for the
announcement –
pronouncement.

Once it was:
"#1 is marrying a Jehovah's Witness;
she won't be celebrating Christmas."

Once it was:
"#3 is gay;
we've asked her to stay away."

Once it was:
"#4 needs a special diet,
so the fridge in the basement is off limits."

Tonight it is:
"#10 is pregnant."

Nothing about #9.

LEGITIMATE

My moment of weakness is nothing
compared to Teresa's.
I let myself be seduced by the want
of a dress.
She let herself be seduced by the want
of what?
Touch, desire, sex, love—
a baby?
Did she want a baby?

"Bastard," Mom calls from the kitchen sink.

"That's harsh, dear. Illegitimate," Dad corrects.

"Bastard. We won't have a bastard in this house," says Mom.

  "No way can she have an abortion," one says.
"That's way worse," one says.
    "No way can she keep it," one says.
"Man, she's barely fourteen," one says.
   "No way can she adopt it away," one says.
 "A Carter in another house— messed up," one says.

"Stop talking about me like I'm not here," Teresa cries,
tears pouring,
voice quivering,
throat hiccupping,
neck reddening.

She stands,
proclaims:
"I am here.
I have a baby inside me.
I made something.
Me.
Not a bastard, Mom.
Not illegitimate, Dad.
Not for any of you to judge.
This is *my* baby.
Mine."

Mom stares daggers at Dad.
The family scatters—
some comforting Teresa;
some taking their leave.

Maybe Teresa
needs
that
baby.

HERITAGE PARK

There is a park
across the street from this house,
a perk of being in the `burbs.

The park is different from the house.
Oh, there are times when kids
nudge for space on the monkey bars,
or fight over swings,
or jeer at falls and scrapes,
but I am not there for that.

As the sun sinks in the sky,
when the kids run home for dinner,
that is when I arrive.

I skip across the grassy field between
our house of chaos and the park of peace,
kick off my shoes,
sink my toes into the sand,
hang from the monkey bars with ease, and
balance on the teeter board
hearing only my giggle
when I fall.

But the best part,
the best part
is swinging and singing.
I swing and sing songs,
songs I make up in the moment
about what I see in this space,
and I sway with the breeze as my accompaniment,
until the setting sun kisses my cheek,
telling me it's time to go home
and
face
the
chaos
once
more.

SEPTEMBER

FIRST DAY OF SCHOOL

#8, #9, and #10 all
go to the same
high school.
Freshman, Sophomore, Senior.
Teresa, Sadie, Faith.

Faith's friends drive; they pick her up.
Teresa and I wait at the bus stop
along with all the other kids
with no one
to drive them.

Brandy whistles.
"Somebody had a hot summer,
Resa.
Heard some South Side guy
knocked you up,
Resa!"

Who's Resa?

"You gotta be careful with those boys
who have vans and weed,
Resa.
Gonna keep it,
Resa?
I bet your parents won't even notice
one
more
kid."

"Shut the f—," Teresa starts.

"Teresa! Don't," I shout-whisper.

"At least I had a man,
Brandy.
Who would even want
to take you into his van,
Brandy?
And, yes! I *am* keeping this kid,
Brandy.
Be a better mom than yours.
That's for sure."

"The bus is here.
Can you shut up and get on the bus?
Brandy's gonna kick our butts,"
I say pulling Teresa away.
"And when did you become *Resa*?"

"*Resa* is what the people who got my back
call me; that's why *you* didn't know.
Are you ever gonna stand up for me, Sister Sadie?
You know nuns can be bad asses, too."

Resa's right about me.
I don't stand— for anything.
And she's right about nuns,
though that's Mother Teresa not Resa.
But she's *not* right about her friends.
They don't have her back.
And that sixteen-year-old
Southsider in the van?
It was a one-night stand.
He doesn't even have a name.

LUNCH CONFESSIONS

"It hurt a little, but I liked it," says Nelly.

"I know— same for me. Shh, here comes Sadie," says Natalia.

"Hey, guys, what's going on?"
I say, pretending I did not hear
what I think I heard.

"Just talking about Nelly's party," says Natalia.

"Sorry you couldn't come, again," says Nelly.

"Yeah, I had a table at Luigi's that stayed
until closing. I wanted to wait for the tip,"
I explain again."How was it?"

Silence.

"Why are you looking at each other?"

Silence.

"Both of you? But we promised to wait…until…"

Holding back tears, I gather my books,
heavy pieces of our fractured promise.
Holding back tears, I inhale in their pity,
exhaling whispers of want dripping in judgment.

"Gotta go, girls. See you at practice," I say, head down.

"Come on, Sadie, stay," says Nelly.

"Come on, Sadie, it's no big deal," says Natalia.

But it is.

HALLWAYS

19 right.
29 left.
9 right.
Nope.
Again.
Again.
Again.

"Need some help with that?" he asks.

"No, thanks," I say.

"Why do you always respond so quickly?
Do you ever say *yes*?" he says.

Dean.

"Not to you,
but I guess you found someone
who would
say
yes."

Dean takes the sticky note
with my locker combo
from my clenched palm
and in one try
opens
my
locker.

"You're welcome,"
he whispers in my ear
before walking down
the hallway to the cafe
to see Natalia.

I slam my locker shut.
19-29-9.
I can open it myself.

THE PSYCHOLOGY OF HAIR

Mr. Manicotti
is not his real name;
it's just what he orders
when he comes into the restaurant
to grade papers and flirt
with Barb, the waitress he is dating.

He wants us to keep a journal as part of our psych grade.
He gives us daily prompts to explore our inner thoughts:
Write about your best part.

I can't, so I write about my worst:

As a little girl, I had wavy hair,
curls bouncing
as I ran through the park,
dangling as I hung upside down from the monkey bars.

And as a little girl, I had— have—
cowlicks
growing in a different direction from the rest,
resisting being combed flat;
my wild locks looked like a lion's mane,
roaring away order
until Mom would say:
"Line up! It's shampoo day."

The youngest girls would
gather on the kitchen floor,
seated cross-legged,
waiting our turn to
be lifted onto the counter,
lay back,
head over the sink,
rest our head in Mom's strong palm,
listen to her bracelet music as she lathered
our locks.

And when it was my turn—
"Tangles!" she'd cry.
And I'd cry
as she fought through my curls
with lather and disgust
as the neat row of sisters
fidgeted in fear.

And then the day came
when the tangles were too much,
too
disruptive.
And so I marched
with #s 10 and 11
and a few bucks
a few blocks—
curls bouncing
as I jumped over
sidewalk cracks
(so as not to break my momma's back).
A mission
to tame the unruly curls

and put an end to tangles.

My curls were cut
into a bowl-shaped coif.
Just like that.

No longer a little girl,
I have learned to fight my cowlicks and curls,
to tame the unruly with
hair dryers and flat irons,
gels and mousses and sprays
that I buy myself.

But when the humidity heightens,
little curls still spring up around my brow.
Smooth tresses begin to frizz,
a wave reappears just at my chin.

A GUEST

Early September practices are hot.
The gym stifling and stinky
with football players taking a break from the sun,
with volleyballers doing sprints and drills,
sneakers squeaking on the sweat drips and drops.

Coach calls, "Sadie, come on over.
I've got great news.
We're moving you to varsity.
They need your height in the middle."

"But that's Faith's team.
This is mine. I mean—
I am part of this, right?" I say.

"And you'll be part of varsity;
here's your new practice jersey."

My whole family is athletic,
everyone had their sport— not me.
I couldn't see in the swimming pool.
I took the softball in the nose, not glove.
I daydreamed on the tennis court;
never understood the score of love.

In junior high, I found volleyball,
but it was more than a sport.
That's where I met
Nelly and Natalia,
learned to be on a team,

learned about girl talk—
make-up, bras, shaving, tampons—
things my sisters kept private,
things my mom neglected to mention.

And now I am going to be a guest
on my sister's team. *Perfect*.

SUNDAY MORNING

Walking home from 7 a.m. mass,
I see Dad sitting on the front steps alone—
cup of tea with three spoonfuls of sugar,
plate of toast heavily buttered,
nail clippers ready to work,
Gregorian chant in
the early fall wind.

"Morning, Dad," I say, interrupting his thoughts.

"Which one are you?
Right, Sadie," he jokes too often.

"Where's your mother?
She said she'd drive you
home."

"She stayed to sing at the nine with Eve," I say.

"Glad she has a friend," he murmurs, reaching for his teacup.

"Dad?" I say.
"Why so many? You had to know
this wouldn't be easy."
He clears his throat;
he sips his tea;
he takes a long look at me
and begins.

HIS REASON

They called me Skippy.
They dressed me, the only child, as a little sailor.
I remember carrying around a baseball glove
waiting for my dad to come home.
And then I carried a paintbrush and glue
to build model cars, trains, and planes, in my room
alone
until high school, where I ran track and sang in the choir.
The choir was not for me.
I would never be on Glee.
In fact, I was asked to leave the risers,
which sort of broke my heart because,
as you know, I love Paul and Art,
and it felt good to be around people.
Track was a better fit.
I'd drift into my mind for a mile or two,
but I was still part of a crew.
Alone. Together.
I guess I just carried a dream of
having a crew of my own—
a family so big no one
would ever have to be
alone.

SUNDAY BRUNCH

"Want breakfast?" he asks.
"And don't say: *No, thanks.*"

A blue bandana covers his blonde locks—
no man-bun today.
Holding up a plate,
cerulean blue eyes plead
through the kitchen window:

"I'm going to stop asking you yes-no questions.
Just eat.
It's a breakfast cal.
You know a calabrese—
pizza dough lovingly
wrapped around
eggs, cheese, pepperoni,
cooked to perfection?"

He's walking away with the plate.
He's coming around to the waitress station.
He's standing in front of me.
He must be 6'4"! Five inches taller than me!

"I'll go get us some grapefruit juice.
See how much better this works
when I don't ask you yes-no questions?
You just have to say: *Thank you.*"

"Thank you," I mutter,
knowing I will pretend to like grapefruit
because
he's
so
cute.

PRACTICE WITH MY "BIG" SIS

Walking into practice
alone,
listening to the team chatter
about summer jobs
and college visits
and the last year of
homecoming court,

and about how Faith
simply can't stand her sisters anymore,
is moving to Arizona after graduation to live with #2,
is on track to be valedictorian,
and just might be homecoming queen with King Frankie,

wishing I wasn't the only sophomore on varsity,
wishing Man-bun was still in high school
(would *he* want go to homecoming— with me?),
wishing *I* was months away from leaving home,
wishing Resa wasn't months away from having a baby.

Whistle.
Line-up for sprints.

Wishing I had eaten lunch,
I tie my hair into a high ponytail,
pull on a headband to control my curls
when I start sweating,
and stand on the line.

OCTOBER

LOSSES

The bus rolls along in the mist.
A chill from a cracked window
blankets the team
in silence.
Another loss.

Street lights flash into our seats—
faces mouthing lyrics,
hands wiping tears,
heads resting on
bags bought by boosters.

Mom's standing among mothers
waiting for Faith and me,
arms in a self-embrace.

Coach guards my exit,
wants to talk,
softly at first:
"Is that your mom over there?
It's been years, since Hope (#3).
Never knew your mom was
so…thin…always…
pregnant."

Nearly nine years of carrying babies in her belly,
not including the miscarriages after #11.

Now more firmly:
"New line up.

You'll ride the bench until
your footwork gets better,
until you and Faith
can work
together."

FOR KEEPS

"I'm keeping it!"
Resa shouts, racing up the stairs,
slamming the bathroom door—
the only bathroom with a working shower.

"What's going on?" I ask,
"I gotta shower before work."

"Teresa and I, well, tonight
we met with Father O'Neill
about
adoption.
I just can't
raise another child
in this house, Sadie.
Your father and I,
we need our time
alone,
together,
to find a way,
to at least try."

"What are you saying, Mom?"

"Teresa is fourteen. Fourteen!
A child. A child
cannot raise
a child!
And I won't do it."

"Why *did*
you do it, Mom?
Why *did*
you want so many of
us?"
I finally say
out loud.

HER REASON

Mom stands at the kitchen sink,
sprinkles the white powder of Comet
until not a speck of steel peeks
and scours with force as she speaks.

I was one of five, one of two daughters
of a Catholic, Italian immigrant.
You never met Grandpa.
The boys were favored and us girls, well,
we had to follow the rules.
I was a good student. Great.
Perfect penmanship and straight A's.
But, still, that was not good enough.
Still I had to earn acclaim, so—
you may not know this—
I became a nun.
It was an acceptable escape.
We'd pray at dawn and scrub the holy floors,
but we also played volleyball
like you and Faith do.
Only we didn't wear those
low-rider spandex shorts of course.
Imagine me spiking in my nun's habit.

Still, it wasn't for me.
It was more rebelling than a calling.
I left the convent young and
met your father shortly after.
We both wanted big families,
a chance to become,
to make what our parents could not.

We'd go dancing and write love letters;
he called me honeybun.

I checked to see if the bathroom was free.
Resa was sitting at the top of the stairs,
her blankie wrapped around her shoulders,
a stuffed elephant by her side.

BELOVED OBJECTS

Mr. Manicotti writes on the board
"beloved: dearly loved, cherished, treasured."
He tells us to journal on our most beloved objects.

I write about the tank dress with sequin detail
that I planned to wear to homecoming
but had to return because I stole it.

I erase that last part.
What if Mr. Manicotti reads this?

I do not have a beloved object,
so I write about Resa's, about Toni's:

Blankie.
As a little girl, Resa (#10) sucked her finger
raw;
she'd soothe herself through
the chaos, sucking and clutching
the pink, satiny border,
draping it around her shoulders
so the border would brush her cheek:

Ellie.
As a little girl, Toni (#11) carried
the stuffed pachyderm
by her trunk or tail
as it were one of her limbs,
fur crusted and tail frayed,
Toni offered Resa Ellie's comfort.

RELAPSE

"Anything else I can bring you?" I ask,
my mind thumping in panic's grasp,
my stomach cramping in defiance,
my eyes haloed in bright lights.

"No, wrap it up. Check, please," I hear.

A half-eaten pizza on the counter,
extra large,
pepperoni,
mushroom,
easy sauce,
cut in
squares.

I shove a piece into my mouth.
And then another.
And then another.

I bend down
to pretend
to tie my shoe
as I swallow.

And then I see
a pair of size fifteens.

"You don't have to steal food, Sadie," he says.
"You'll never go hungry now that you're here."

HOMECOMING

Faith is homecoming queen.
She wears a pink tank dress (no sequins)
paid for with hours of kneading dough
at the bakery.
She looks beautiful.

I work
slinging pizzas and pitchers
to groups of teens—
wilted wrist corsages,
surreptitiously reattaching fake eyelashes,
suited beaus
using forks and knives to cut their slices
so no sauce drips on their new duds.

"Didn't you want to go?
Scratch that.
Why didn't you go?"
he asks, pushing my order
through the heated window.

"No money for a dress.
My sisters' hand-me-downs
are all too small.
I'm a giant if you haven't noticed."

"Oh, I noticed," he winks.
"So no one asked you, huh?" he grins.

"Let's just say I've got other priorities.
Saving up for a car,"
I say,
thinking *my escape plan*,
thinking *a sanctuary of my own.*

All summer, I thought I'd go
to homecoming with Dean,
who's Faith's age,
who's Frankie's friend.
She would have hated a double-date.
But Dean broke up with me
because I didn't say *yes.*
But Natalia did.

"Right.
So serious.
Serious Sadie.
Well, Serious,
your pizza's up."

STOP THE CLOCKS

My English teacher
taps her French manicured nails
on the ancient black board
to teach us stress management
during high stakes tests.

Identify the hyperbole in Auden's "Funeral Blues."

Tap. My eyes ache.
Tap. My brow throbs.
Tap. My heartbeat rises.
Tap. To my throat.
Tap. Into my nose.
Tap. Behind my aching eyes.
Tap. Under my throbbing brow.

The second hand on the wall clock
ticks like a fire alarm,
tocks like a dripping faucet.

I want the tap, tapping to silence.
I want the tick, tocking to stop.

Tap, tick. Tock, tap.

Every sound resonates
in the space between
my scalp and my skull.

The tapping stops.
My test covered in dots.
Not one bubble filled.

"Sadie? Another headache?" she says.

Tick, tock.

TEAM PARTY

MVP went to Faith—
a certificate
of appreciation
for her leadership.

She gives a short speech
about hard work,
about balancing
practice and games
with
school and work,
about not having much time for
fun or family,
about how the girls on the team
are like her
sisters.

Coach
shares the stats:
the most kills— Faith
the most digs— Faith
the most blocks— Faith.

"We're sorry to see our seniors go.
Juniors? Sadie? We have our work
cut out for us next year. See you at
summer camp."

Barb brings the team
three large pizzas and
three pitchers of pop.

Coach sits next to me:
"I know this wasn't an easy season
for you—
being younger,
in your sister's shadow.
Maybe I didn't do enough
team building.
Maybe I didn't push you.
Maybe you weren't ready.
Maybe next year,"
she says, standing to fill her plate.

Maybe.

Barb brings me
a glass of grapefruit juice,
a register receipt that says,
"Don't look so serious.
Smile, Sadie."

And I do.

TWENTY-SOMETHING WEEKS

At the bus stop,
Resa tells Brandy
that the baby
is the size of a
banana,
kicks and jabs the walls of her womb,
picks up sounds,
is hearing now,
sways and swoons to Dad's car tunes
on rides to the doc.
Simon and Garfunkel are his? her? favorite.

At the bus stop,
I witness the crowd
surrounding Resa
to hear the stories of her
baby growing.
I witness Resa
glowing.

She will not give this baby away.

NOVEMBER

COMING HOME

At Thanksgiving, we actually set the picnic table:
tablecloth, china, stemware, linen napkins.
Nothing matches, but it looks like
a nice place to give thanks
for the turkey donated by the church,
for the siblings who made their way home,
and will now make it even harder to use the shower.

At Thanksgiving, my mom actually cooks again:
baskets of crescent rolls,
pans of mashed potatoes,
sparkling grape juice to toast,
a turkey hacked to bits with the electric knife,
and bowls of the best Italian sausage stuffing.

She's puts the turkey in at dawn
before heading off to 7:00 a.m. mass,
and we wake to the heavenly smell of
food.

When the bird is ready, #3 arrives.
A surprise.
Once banished for her sins,
Dad and Mom have forgiven, now welcome
Hope and her partner, Maggie,
to this family dinner.

A meal:
atonement for our sin,
rejecting her for who she loves,
banishing her from a seat at our dysfunctional table.

Dad says, "Let's pray."

We say, "Bless us, oh Lord, for these thy gifts."

We don't say, "Bless us, Hope, for we have sinned."
We don't say, "Bless us, Resa, for we will love your kin."
We don't say, "Bless Dad with a job."

We just eat the hacked turkey in silence.

And I think:
Here we all are
sitting side by side
alone
together.
Beloved objects
my parents
wanted
but
don't
know
how
to
treasure.

DESSERT

Banana cream,
French silk,
apple,
pumpkin,
pecan.
Pies.
Hope's partner brought us pies.

I begin to cut a slice of banana cream for Dad
when I hear,
"Can I help you with that?
Scratch that.
You clearly need help."

"Dad," Hannah (#7) says,
"You remember my boyfriend,
Aaron?
And this is Sam.
He's Aaron's friend.
Used to live just down the street,
went to our church,
works with Sadie.
Sadie?
You remember
Sam,
right?"

Hannah's wearing a clever grin.

SAM

"Hello, everyone.
Thanks for having me.
My parents
sold our house this summer
to travel America in their RV.
They invited me
sort of.
Figured I'd give them their space
and get my own place.
Made my own Cornish hen today,
but it was
kind of lonely," Sam says,
eyes darting around.

"Hey, that's some table.
You know, at church
we'd see your family
take up an entire pew.
My mom always wondered
what your dinner table was like—
how you fed so many kids, Mr. Carter, sir.
Hey, check out those benches—
look like church pews.
So cool.
I'm an only child.
And…I'm…
rambling now.
How about some pie?"

Adorable.

"Slice of banana cream, please," Dad says to Sam
holding out a plate, no side of grin.
"French silk for me," says Resa.
"Pumpkin, with Cool Whip," says Toni.
"Pumpkin is my favorite, too," winks Sam.

Toni swoons.

"None for me. I gotta get to the bakery for black Friday's rush,"
says Faith.

"Anyone else?" say Sam's blue eyes
pleading
with
me.

"Pecan pie," I say.

Because this is nuts.

AFTER PIE

I'm tucked
in the worn tweed
of the sofa
between Sam and Hannah.
Football highlights bounce
off the mirrored wall
through the darkness.
Resa and Toni doze
on the carpet
with Blankie and Ellie.
Older siblings catch up
with high school friends
at the bar.
Dad in the garage.
Mom in the kitchen
eating pie in peace.
Sam's wrist rests against mine.
I can see a shiny scar
from oven burns.
He inches his fingers
under mine,
then waits,
as if asking.

I do not say *no, thanks.*
And I pretend to watch
football.

SLEEP OVER

I actually do have good friends
who get me.

If Nelly said we need a girls night,
she knows I'd say
no, thanks
to crowds, dressing up, fake eyelashes, boys.
Exhausting.

So she plans a good old-fashioned sleepover:
popcorn, jammies, a real bed, and a funny movie.
Relaxing.

In eighth grade, we went to a graduation sleepover.
The movie was *The Exorcist*,
which was a strange choice since most of us are Christian.

I spent all of the movie
in the kitchen,
talking to the mom,
trying to block out the screams
except for the part where I brought popcorn to Nelly.

I spent all of the night
in a corner,
fighting off nightmares,
trying to unsee Linda Blair's head spinning.

Tonight,
Pitch Perfect works out well for me.
I sleep soundly on Nelly's trundle.
Mash-ups beat spinning heads any day.

MANICOTTI'S MASLOW LECTURE

"Journal for five
about what you need to survive.
Go."

I'm not in the mood,
so I make a list:
food, blanket, door that locks.

Mr. Manicotti changes the slide
to reveal Maslow's Hierarchy of Needs.

Self-Fulfillment Needs

Actualization
purpose, meaning, acceptance, creativity

Psychological Needs

Belongingness
intimacy, friends, love, family, sense of connection
Esteem
prestige, accomplishment, confidence

Basic Needs

Physiological
food, water, shelter, clothing, sleep
Safety
security, stability, health, employment

He proceeds:"The human brain is driven by a basic need to
survive; basic needs are the basis to build the hierarchy,
but here's the problem:

none of these needs can be met without social connection. We must connect physically and emotionally if we are to survive. We need to work together for the basics so we can find our purpose."

I raise my hand.

"What happens
to a person
who grows up
without
the love
of his parents?
Can he
self
actualize?"

The bell rings.

THREE LITTLE GIRLS

went
camping
with their father
when he had a job.

"Are we really going to sleep on the roof of the van?" asked
Teresa.

"Yes, so that we can see the constellations, so that the stars can
catch our dreams," said Dad.

"What if I fall?" asked Toni. "The stars can't catch me if Sadie or
Teresa kick me off."

"Oh, no worries, little one. I have bungee cords to hold your
sleeping bags in place," said Dad.

An end-of-summer camping trip
to celebrate Toni's entry to elementary,
to give Mom a weekend of peace,
to give Dad time to bond after a long work week.

The shadows of the trees trembled,
making glimmer the patient constellations.
Toni reached her hands for the stars.
Teresa reached, too.
Their fingers danced with the branches,
flickers of fireflies blossomed between.
I reached across to give the girls a squeeze;
it was a beautiful scene.
And then, we waited for our dreams.

THREE LITTLE GIRLS

go
to church
with their mother
when she was feeling motherly.

7:00 a.m. mass:
a solemn service,
no song,
just prayer.
Genuflect
at the first pew,
middle aisle,
kneel,
chin resting on
praying palms.

I no longer
hear
the readings;
I just respond:
"Lord have mercy."
"Thanks be to God."
"Alleluia."
"Amen."
"Grant us peace."

This little girl
half kneels, half sits
leaning her butt on the pew
a little being in her blessed belly.

This little girl
digs into her jeans pocket,
pulling out a few coins
for the church's offering basket.

And this little girl
watches her mom—
chin on prayered palms,
bracelets near elbows,
eyes closed
deep in prayer.

A tear.

OPEN ADOPTION

Mom does not rise
from her knees,
though Resa has to pee.

We wait for Father O'Neill.
Resa thinks it is to discuss
if the church will baptize the babe.
Mom knows it is to meet
parents for the being in the belly.

"This is Mr. and Mrs. Blindside,
Resa.
Open adoption.
College education.
Good family.
Won't want for anything."

"How could you, Mom?"

Three little girls
walk away from church.

"What's an open adoption
even mean?"
Toni asks, pulling on her hat.

"It means Resa can keep in touch—
letters, pictures, a call or text,
maybe visit over the years,"
I explain offering Hannah's scarf,
which I *borrowed,* to Resa.

"I can't give up
this being
growing within me—
3 pounds of him-her,
a pint and half of
amniotic fluid
that my body made
to protect him.
See, I'm studying,"
Resa drops to her knees
upon frozen leaves
and so do we.

"I still gotta pee."

DECEMBER

REPAYING DEBTS

The trunk of the car does not have bags of food:
no milk for the cereal,
no bread for lunches,
no dried pasta or sauce,
certainly no Pop-Tarts.

The trunk of the car does have one box:
granulated sugar,
evaporated milk,
bags of chocolate chips,
vanilla,
chopped walnuts.

Mom's making fudge.
It's her way to
pay
for all the favors,
for all the delays,
for all the overdrafts
and the extra cash
that got us
through
the
year.

There was a time that Mom made cookies,
around the time I was hiding Pop-Tarts,
but we'd eat every buttery, golden ounce.
Now she puts nuts in the fudge,
so we don't
gorge ourselves on gratitude,
but I like nuts.

COOKIE CONFESSIONAL

You were not made for me.

Carefully measured ingredients
joining each other
in grandma's mixing bowl,
the wooden spoon working you into a sweet, floury dough.
Sugar and butter are folded into the crumbs
until they became one:
you.

The hands that gently separated you into perfectly round pillows
and then delivered you to a warm oven
were my mother's.
As the butter in you melted,
the savory smell wafted through the house,
and those smells brought me to the oven to see
you
turn that beautiful brown.
And as you cooled on the rack,
you
danced in the powdery white sugar,
the sugar that gave you your beautiful glow.

And then you were delivered into the shiny cookie tins
and sealed for gifts.

No, you were not made for me.

But I could not forget you.
As I watched TV or did my homework
I thought of you
resting in that powdered sugar,
sealed in the cookie tin,
hidden away from the children.

And so when no one was around,
I crept in and gently, quietly uncovered one tin
and then another.

There was no time to marvel at your beauty.
I just popped you into my mouth,
savoring the buttery taste,
then licking my lips to hide the evidence.

And so when no one is around,
I creep in and gently, quietly peak under the bed,
but there are no tins of fudge with nuts
just shopping bags:
pots,
pans,
plates,
mugs,
frames,
vases.

TREE TRIMMING

There was a time
when we strapped a pine
to the roof of the Sportabout.

There was a time
when the phonograph
exhaled "Frosty" and "Drummer Boy."

There was a time
when Mom ogled ornaments
crafted by the hands of her babes.

There was a time
when we assembled a spruce from a box,
when the phonograph went silent,
when the ornaments became a chore.

Last year, we simply set the spurious spruce
in the patio alongside the rusty bikes;
we didn't even bother to remove the lights.

This year, as I vacuum spider webs from the branches,
siblings emerge from basements and bathrooms
to adorn fake needles with treasured trinkets,
to illuminate a string of lights,
to hum "Silent Night"
together.

THE MORN' BABY JESUS IS BORN

No setting the picnic table today
with mismatched china and glasses.
Mom's gone to sing in the choir— all the masses.
Dad's left behind to explain the empty stockings.

"Can't afford it," he says.

"What about Christmas dinner?" I ask.

"Can't afford it," he says. "We're going to Hope and Maggie's."

"And what about all those bags under your bed?"

"Those were Eve's," Dad says. "Mom was holding them for her,
hiding them from Eve's kids until Christmas."

He puts on the tea,
pops in some toast,
drops the needle on Gregorian Chant,
and takes a seat in the rocking chair
next to the fake tree,
adorned with homemade
ornaments from a time when we
cut stars, glued yarn, and proudly
pasted our portraits for display.

"Come on," Resa says.
"Let's borrow some eggs from next door
and make French toast;
we're starving."

GIFTS OF STONES

I have a memory of Christmas.
We each received a robe— different colors.
Eight girls and three boys sat with wrapped boxes
of the same shape and size.
After the first one was opened,
we all knew what we had gotten.

I have a memory of Christmas.
We each received an item of jewelry— different stones.
Eight girls and three boys (perhaps there were fewer that year)
sat with wrapped boxes of the same shape and size.
After the first one was opened,
we all knew what we had gotten,
but this was a bit different.

The jewelry told a story of our birth.
Amethyst, Pearl, Ruby, Sapphire, Topaz, Turquoise.
Stones.
I learned that mine was an emerald.
I was-am the only
emerald
stone.

CHRISTMAS NIGHT

In the living room,
I'm tucked
between Hannah and Faith,
snuggling on Hope's sofa
beside a cozy fire,
under a blanket,
sipping on Baileys
in safe silence.

In the dining room,
the three of them
are sitting at the table
with pie and bourbon.

"It's three months away.
Mom won't yet accept the baby,
and you have the space,"
Dad says.

"We don't know what to say,"
sighs Hope, eyes asking Maggie.

"We'll take the baby," says Maggie,
"but not without Resa."

LIFE BEYOND THE CARTERS

Around the holidays each year,
Godmother takes me away
from Lilac Lane
to her Rogers Park place.

She used to pick me up
in her yellow VW bug,
but she says this year I am old enough
to meet her at Union Station.

We take the "L" north,
fight the wind a few blocks
to her place by the lake.
She makes tea, crumbles some granola,
lets me shower uninterrupted,
shares her Clinique lotions,
teaches me to meditate through headaches,
cracks the window so I can hear the waves
while I sleep.

We lunch in The Walnut Room—
once Field's, now Macy's,
sip hot chocolate beside the 45-foot tree,
run through the roster of siblings.

She shows me pictures from her travels
where in Paris she climbed the Eiffel Tower,
where in Spain she sunbathed seaside,
where in Mexico she prepared *La Rejunta*,
where in Poland she witnessed Auschwitz.
She pulls out a glossy annual report—
the bread and butter of freelance journalism.
I read her words and pics telling stories
of lives lived.
She passes me a Parisian scarf,
tells me I am *très chic*.
She pays the bill;
I pay the tip.

We stroll State Street towards Union Station.
Godmother threads her arm with mine
comforting with a knowing tug
as we glide through slush
and brave the winds of Chicago
together.

SHAMEFUL PRIDE

I tuck my new scarf under my sweater
as I kick off my boots.

        "What did she get you?" Toni asks.
"Did you have dessert?" Resa asks.
      "Still doing annual reports?" Dad asks.
          "How's the freelance working out?"

Faith changes the channel on the TV.
Mom glances up from the kitchen sink.
Hannah rushes over to ask about the lotion.

Of the twenty-two godparents,
I got the best one.
Dad met her at work,
a young photojournalist,
single,
Catholic,
who would babysit.

And then I was born,
and she was so kind
and Catholic
and willing
to put in the time.

By the teens, most godparents
drift away;
relationships with parents change,
no *in loco parentis* needed,
but this godmother,
she's stuck around
for me.

A gift
just for
Me.

TIPS

Thirty George Washingtons.
Two Alexander Hamiltons.
Ten Abraham Lincolns.
Stacked neatly,
ready for deposit.

Holiday parties
equal
good tips
equal
better used car.

I roll up my apron,
zip my parka,
march across the street,
access the bank lobby,
deposit my double shift,
and start the walk home.

Solitude at last—
don't even mind the cold.

The white clouds of my breath
are my only companion
until I feel a car slow,
until I hear the window lower,
until I look over and see
Sam.

"This is creepy," I say.

"I know, but it's not safe.
Let me take you the rest of the way."

In the two minute drive,
I'm wondering if he'll kiss me
and wondering what it will feel like
if he does.

"Nice Christmas?" he asks.

"Yeah, it was okay," I say.
"You were in Florida, right?
With your parents? How nice."

"Yeah, but Santa and palm trees?
Now that's creepy," he says.

Sam stops at the end
of the driveway,
a car's idling,
two people inside
close.

Mom gets out.
The car reverses.
Sam pulls in.

 "Who was that?" he asks.

"I don't know."

GHOSTS

I'm listening to the sounds
of *A Christmas Carol* on TV
drifting toward the front door

knowing that Resa and her being
are nestled in the torn tweed
unable to sleep again,

knowing that Mom and her secret
are shuffled off to bed
unable to utter truth yet,

knowing the ghosts of Present
haunt our home
and not knowing the ghosts Yet to Come.

I take off my shoes,
unzip my parka,
toss my apron down the basement stairs,
re-wrap my new scarf—
infinity—
and sit among the ghosts.

NEW YEAR'S INVITATION

Nelly and Natalia
stare at me
across the pick-up counter,
cute infinity scarves
draped around their adorable necks.

"You are coming! No excuses."

"Can't you see? I am working.
Notice the red t-shirt?
Notice the black apron?
This is not New Year's Eve attire."

"Hey, Sam, what time do you close?"

"Hey, rude girls, eleven,
but Sadie won't be here that late.
She's not closing."

"Thanks, Sam," I roll my eyes his way.
He rolls his eyes with a smile to mine.
"But really— I don't even know how
to have fun anymore.
And I don't have a ride.
And I'm not asking Faith."

"Oh, Sam?" calls Natalia.

"Don't. Don't even!" I plead.

MY RIDE

opens my door for me,
turns the key,
top-forty countdown blasts,
fingers reach for the volume
at the same time.

"Why isn't it cold in here?" I say.

"I warmed it up while you were
checking out," Sam says.
"Where to?"

"Home?" I wish, thinking how sweet
that he warmed up the car for me-us.

"No way. You need to
do high school stuff,
drink with your girls,
have some fun,
put Serious Sadie
on hold,
but I gotta make a pit stop first."

On the ten minute drive,
I'm wondering if he'll kiss me
and wondering what it will feel like
if he does.

Sam starts to sing
at the top of his lungs—
a little out of key.
He knows every word—
every pause.

I smile suddenly aware:
the seat belt—
a gentle hug across my chest,
the heated seats—
a blanket for my bum,
the number one song of the year—
whatever Sam is singing.

A WITNESS

A giant stands in the center of the patio.
Once a sapling carried home
in a white Styrofoam cup,
dirt packed by the hands
of third-grade Sam.
The now four-story tree sways
with the winter wind,
"Welcome home, Sam."

Sam has taken me to meet his tree,
to see his childhood home,
to hear his story
on this New Year's Eve.

"Dad wooed Mom," he begins.
"He was a cop moonlighting,
a security guard at Carson's.
Mom already married with a son.
Dad already married with three.
Crazy about each other.
They started a life together
and then had me.
I planted this tree."

A little boy stands at the patio door,
frost framing his face.

"Hey, maybe the kid will climb your tree someday," I say.

"Maybe," Sam says, pulling my scarf to my chin
so close I can feel his breath.
"Now let's get you to your party.
Remember?
Fun?"

PARTY GIRL

Walking into the party
alone,
I pull my parka closed
hugging myself,
reassuring myself,
convincing myself,

that this is a good idea,
that I am capable of fun,
that I can make small talk,
that I will laugh.

My first stop is Nelly's room
to raid her closet for something cute.
She's half my height,
so a cute top is the best I can do.
Perfume to cover the pizza remains.
Product to calm the frizz.
Lip gloss?
Yes.
Fun Sadie needs gloss.

Walking into Nelly's basement,
I see twenty teens,
pool and ping pong,
Navy Pier countdown,
make-out sessions,
quarters and beer.
Nelly hands me a cue
and whispers,
"Glad you're here.
We got next game."

JANUARY

NEW YEAR'S DAY LECTURE

Nelly's PJ pants are way too short,
but a cozy quilt warms
my ankles
as we sit on her
leather sofas,
Diet Cokes and bagels,
party remains
scattered about.

I only hear every other word
about Dean being a jerk,
about parents too strict,
about spring break trips,
and college visits
until the lecture begins.

Nelly: Earth to Sadie! Where do you go?

Me: I'm thinking about Faith going to college soon.

Natalia: Maybe you will get her room? It's bigger than that
corner box you sleep in.

Me: Maybe. And Hannah moving out to move in with Aaron.

Nelly: Oh, snap, living in sin!

Me: It's going to kill my parents. They've lost all control:
a Jehovah's marriage, lesbian love, teenage pregnancy, now living
in sin.

Nelly: Oh, and do not forget: you are a pilferer, Sister Sadie! Oh, the shame.

Natalia: Ouch, don't joke. That was back in August. At least she's still a virgin.

Me: Thank you, Natalia. And, by the way, I confessed about the dress. Absolved officially but forever tainted.

Nelly: Sadie, you have to stop with these rules.

Me: Commandments.

Nelly: Commandments for what? To reject fun, love, family? What about hopes? Dreams? You think going to confession can undo what you did to your sister?

Natalia: Wait! Which one?

Nelly: Hope! And you think your mom going to church can make up adopting out her grandchild?

Natalia: Wait! Which one?

Nelly: Teresa's baby, Natalia. Try to keep up. Sadie, your mom should try going to a few volleyball games— maybe take Teresa to her birthing class. And your dad, asking you guys to pay rent instead of getting a job himself? My God, your parents!

Natalia: Preach, sister!

Me: You're right. It's effed up. But, geesh, how do you know all this stuff?

Nelly: Faith told my sister, but I wish you would have trusted us. We'll listen if you just let us.

Me: Well, there is one more thing. My mom might be having an affair.

BACK TO SCHOOL

When we return from break,
Mr. Manicotti gives us a survey,
tells us for the term we'll be
exploring personality.
First up: Empaths.

He asks us five questions
to which I cannot reply *no, thanks*
to even one:

One.
Are you emotionally drained by crowds,
need time alone to revive?
Two.
Do you avoid being at the center,
prefer to stay on the perimeter?
Three.
Do your nerves get frayed,
sounds, smells cause you distress?
Four.
Are you highly sensitive to others' emotions,
taking on their anger, sadness, joy?
Five.
Do you feel physically or emotionally ill when watching violent
images in movies or TV?

When we complete the survey,
Jonathan raises his hand and says,
"What's the opposite of an empath?
Because none apply to me.
I love slasher movies."

Mr. Manicotti simply says,
"A psychopath.
But don't worry, Johnny boy.
There's still hope for you."

BEHIND THE WHEEL

In May, I'll turn sixteen,
and that means
a license to drive,
to buy a car,
to go where I please,
see new places,
escape the chaos,
be
alone.

Drivers Ed. is a zero period class,
which begins an hour before first
at 7:00 a.m., but there's no bus.

Mom agrees to drive me the two miles to school.

Since Teresa started showing, Mom
started going to St. Pius for 7:00 a.m. mass.
It's Eve's parish, and it's closer to school.

I wonder if she is ashamed to show her face at Ascension.
I wonder if she is avoiding Father O'Neill's condemnation,
but I don't ask.

I'm just happy Mom has a friend.
I'm just happy to not have to trek
through Chiberia for driving lessons.

At the end of our block,
Mom spots

a figure leaning into the wind
cinnamon Afro frosting at the tips with snow.

"Is that Brandy Kalu?" she asks.
"She must be…"

"My drivers ed partner," I say.

"Let's give her a ride.
It's the Christian thing to do, right?" Mom says.

Like cheating on your husband, I think.

"Thanks," Brandy says, sniffling.
"Dad's working second shift
at Ferrara; he gets home at six—
can't wake him, but, hey, all the
Lemonheads and Red Hots I can eat."

"No problem. Bring me some Lemonheads,
and you've got a ride to drivers ed,
until it warms up at least," Mom says.

"Great," I say, adjusting my scarf.

DEAR BRANDY

@eight
Long, blond hair whips side to side as a spinning drum—
for volume,
pageant dresses that would fit a pencil,
Velcro in place along the back,
a hand-held mirror snaps into the plastic palm,
a tanned beau and brunette friend—
"Bring your Barbies," you'd say, and I would.
Packed them up in a paper bag
then trekked across Timber Hollow
for a summer play date.
Together, we imagined a world for our plastic posse.

@ten
A lip-sync number to New Edition's "Candy Girl"—
with tumbling,
matching pink track suits,
a hand-held mirror mimics a microphone,
a boom box plays the compact disc—
"Let's try out for the talent show," you said, and I tried.
Practiced every day after school in your basement
but fainted at the tryout.
Together, we imagined a world where people cheered for us.

@twelve
Short maroon and white skirts glide across the gym floor—
with poms,
band in the stands, coaches and clubs on display,
a junior high pep rally to welcome the sevvies,
an invitation to be a cheerleader, jock, or band geek—
"Let's try out for cheerleading," you said, and I did,
but you made the squad, and I didn't,
and you made fun of the goodie goodies, while I became one,
and we were no longer an us.

MERGING

A tall boy with light brown shaggy hair,
almost-skinny brown jeans,
and a navy Canada Goose jacket
leans against our assigned
blue Ford Taurus.

"Uh, good morning," he says.
"Guess we're all going to learn to drive
together. Yay, parallel parking."

"I already know how to drive," says Brandy.
"My mom taught me last summer in New York."

Brandy's lying, but I stay quiet.

"Great. I have no clue," he says.
"My mom won't let me near the keys.
She calls me Hapless Henry—
not that I'll be bad luck or anything."

"Great," says Brandy rolling her eyes.

Henry Lucas.

I was 5'9" in eighth grade.
Every boy was too short
back then,
but Henry was the shortest,
and he had a crush on me.

At lunch in junior high,
I'd sit in the corner,
with books of lives
beyond my own.
When I read or write,
only that world exists.

I'd lose time,
deaf to the discord.

One day, when the bell rang
me back to bedlam,
on the table
melted an ice cream sandwich
with a sticky note:
Will you go out with me? Henry.

I didn't have the heart to say *no, thanks.*
I guess I was a heightist,
but I ate-slurped every ice cream sandwich
Henry sent my way
until *he* went away.

But now, here he is.
Abercrombie Fitch
meets
Harry Potter
in
Hapless Henry Lucas.
I'd like to get under his
Canada Goose cloak.

"Ah, I see you've all met.
I think this will be a fun
group. Don't you, Sadie?"
says Mr. Manicotti,
dangling the keys.

SIRENS AND ICE CREAM

Faith, Resa, Toni, and I are in the basement.
Hannah is on a date with Aaron, again.
We hear a glass shatter
in the stainless steel sink,
then another.

Their talk over
gin and tonics
turned hostile.

We hear the sirens go off:
Mom's tongue stings.
Dad's fists pound.
We know this will go on.

Resa says, "Let's get out of here. Baby needs ice cream."

We watch her
waddle up the stairs in her slippers,
ankles swollen,
gently turn the knob to the garage door—
stealthy skill—
wave us all through.

She
rolls her eyes at the canoe,
pushes Faith from the driver's side, says
"Ain't no way I'll fit in the back.
Can't get in on that side either
because of that stupid canoe."

She
plops into the seat butt first,
pulls down the visor for the keys,
opens the garage door,
turns the engine, once, twice, and then
into reverse for ice cream.

"She knows how to drive?" I say from back.

"You don't?" she says, eyes rolling into the rearview mirror.

She has even more sass pregnant.

"I just *started* drivers ed," I say.

"We sneak out in the car several times a week," Resa reveals.

"We don't ask you to come because, well..." says Toni
reaching for the tassels on my scarf.

"Because you'll judge and...you're no fun," says Faith.

When we get to the convenience store,
where we've always gone for
milk, eggs, bread,
Faith ponies up a few bucks
for two pints—
cookie dough and red velvet.
Four spoons.

We sit in the car
passing pints
waiting for
sirens
to
subside.

MID-WEEK SHIFT

When Barb calls in sick,
Luigi asks me to pick up her shift.
Mr. Manicotti is sitting
at table nineteen
grading papers
waiting for Barb to order
when I arrive and say,
"The usual?"

"Ah, Sadie," he says
not a hint of surprise in his eyes,
"just looking at your survey,
and I gotta say
you have a gift
in a way.
Take a seat."

"I really gotta prep
the antipasti," I say.

"That can wait. Sit."

And so begins the lecture:

"I've known your family
for a decade and have
witnessed your past.
Faith was in this very class.

"But you are not Faith.
She has built a shield
to deflect the pain,
to protect her heart.
And she's learned
when
to take it down.

"But you, you absorb
all the chaos, depression,
anger, rejection, as if it were yours
alone.

"You don't know how
to assuage the pain,
to lean on others.
And it has taken its
toll.
Their anger is not yours.
Their sadness is not yours.
Their choices are not yours.
But you are
their daughter,
their sister,
their friend."

"So, manicotti?" I say.
And walk away.

MIRROR, MIRROR

And now I am
crying,
rushing to the bathroom
for toilet paper to wipe away
the sting.

I lock the door
to lecture the specter
in the mirror:

Asking for food when the cupboards are bare,
asking for healing when no salve exists,
asking for affection when it's been drained,
asking for time when the last second's been sapped,
asking for acceptance when it's already been withheld—
it leads to rejection.

You couldn't survive that.

Get your needs met on your own.
Keep yourself safe on your own.
Who needs belonging?
You have family, friends, not-quite boyfriends
just
at
a
distance.
Okay, are we good? Yes?

Mirror shakes her head.

PRAYING ALONE

My first communion teacher, Sister Mary Thomas,
said, "Prayer is the bridge between panic and peace."

It is from Sister Mary Thomas
that I learned to
quiet the flutters in my heart,
slow the quivers in my breath
through prayer.
Maybe that's why I took to church
more than
the others.

I remember telling her
that I didn't know what to say,
that I really didn't know how to pray.
I just memorized mass,
recited the psalms and creeds.

I remember her telling me:
Take comfort in words you repeat and psalms you sing
until your own lines and verses emerge.
Take comfort in silence, too,
and let prayer find you.

That was about the time when I started attending mass
on my own.

When Dad had a job,
we'd attend the ten-thirty.
It was the mass with music,
the mass to be seen,
the mass followed by a donut social.

One time, we were all packed into the cars (plural)
waiting for Mom, and I felt the flutters and quivers.
Dad told me to start walking, get some air,
but my family didn't come.

I sat in the back.
I prayed on my own.
I ate three donuts with powdered sugar.
I loved the solitude and peace.
I was alone,
but I was not lonely.

They showed up for the noon mass.
I waved powdered-donut fingers at them
as they drove past me as I walked home
in peace.

FEBRUARY

HEART-SHAPED PIZZA FOR TWO

Happy Valentine's Day!
Order a heart-shaped pizza,
and our cooks will write a
special message in tomato sauce.

It's really cute actually.

Mr. Manicotti is standing at the front counter
in a wool navy suit, burgundy tie,
light pink shirt with handkerchief.
Barb comes to the front, says hi,
hands him not manicotti-to-go
but a large pizza box.

"Can you make sure it's the right one?" he says.

"Sure," she says.

Will you marry me? is scribed in tomato sauce,
and when she looks up,
Mr. Manicotti is on one knee with a ring.

MORE HEARTS

Once it slows, I order a li'l pizza,
a 5" baby pizza for myself.
Sam makes it heart-shaped,
and I ask for the rest of it,
wanting my money's worth.
Just before he passes it through,
he picks up the tomato-sauce squeeze bottle
and writes,
Happy V-Day!

I hear a bell at the front counter
just as I am about to take a bite.

"Is Sam here?" she asks looking past
me into the kitchen, tapping her French-manicured nails
on the plastic menu.

"Hey," Sam says, pushing open the
door. "What's up, Miranda?"

Miranda?

"Traci's having an anti-Valentines party,
you know, for those of us without sweethearts.
Want to come by after work?"

"Sure, text me the address.
Give me your phone," he says.

And I watch, mouth agape,

as he reaches for her phone,
as his dough-manicured nails
tap his number into her contacts.

"Thanks," she says to me as she leaves.

Happy V-Day! says my li'l heart-shaped pizza.

LOVERS' PARADISE

Nelly and Natalia have a plan
to go on the St. Pius Youth Group spring break,
invite Dean and Donnie,
swap rooms,
vacation like lovers
in the glorious hotels of
Wisconsin Dells.

They have a month to get bikini ready:
baking in tanning beds,
X90-whatevering workouts,
dieting with hot sauce and lemons.

They ask if I want to come—
can ask a guy
if I want,
but we'd need another couple
to do the swap;
can room with what's-her-name
if I want;
can afford it with as much as I work
if I want;
can use a tan and some fun,
that I desperately need.

I decline.
No, thanks.
Just months away
from my license and a car,
saving every penny,
but I would like to see
Sam
shirtless,
surfing
the Kalahari wave pool.

PARALLEL PARKING

Mr. Manicotti has a sub,
so we have to draw a cartoon strip of
parallel parking instead of actually
driving.

"So where have you been, Henry?" says Brandy. "You just never
came back after winter break in eighth grade. And here you are
for drivers ed— only you don't go to school *here*. What's up?"

   "Brandy, maybe he wants to keep it private," I say outlining the
   frames. "You don't have to tell us if you don't want to, Henry."

"Thanks, Sadie, but I don't mind," Henry says, sketching the car
positions. "You always were direct, Brandy. I appreciate that."

"See, Sadie. You should try it sometime. I know you are just
dying to know," says Brandy, looking at her phone.

   "Shh, Brandy. Let him talk," I say, coloring the cars in the third
                              frame, navy for Henry's jacket,
                                   red for my scarf,
                                   pink for my gloves.

"I'm homeschooled. That winter in eighth grade? My mom had a
breakdown, freaked out about leaving the house, fell into a deep
depression. Dad thought it would be best if I stayed home to
keep an eye on her; he's a lawyer— never home."

"That sucks, Henry, about your mom, but at least you don't have
to go to school," says Brandy looking up from a text.

"I actually like coming to your school—"

Did he glance at me?

"But this is sort of your break, right? From your mom, being in
the house? And driving's gotta feel so liberating, knowing
you can get away?"
I say.

"Yep, you get me, Sadie," says Henry as he begins to color the
final frame of our parallel parking cartoon. "Hey, the cars match
us. Nice."

ALMOST FULL TERM

Resa stops coming to school—
belly too big,
ankles too swollen,
hallways too nosy.

She reclaims her birth name, Teresa,
as a sign of her motherhood maturity—
after all, eight pounds of baby
rest just under her enormous breasts.

Teresa cries all the time,
but she explains her baby cannot;
tear ducts don't develop
until after the first month.

Teresa tells me her friends are beotches—
not one has come by to visit,
except Brandy.

I'm silent,
offering tissues and tea
as she completes packets
for English and History
at the picnic table.

"So tell me about Sam," she says.
"And Henry. This stuff is so boring.
Brandy says Henry's super cute
that he likes you— a lot.
You're so lucky to be skinny.
I hate you, you know,"
she says checking out her
profile in the patio window.
"All *that* and you don't want to work it."

I get up to turn on the kettle.

"Now *I* can work it.
Had guys all over me last summer.
And look at me now.
Disgusting.
You better be worth it, little one."

And I wonder if that little one
will be
treasured.

NIGHTMARES

I sit on my side, needing to cough,
bring my hand to my mouth to stifle the sound,
and when I pull my hand away,
I see three pearls resting in my palm.
Dazed, I feel my way to the bathroom
in the dark,
flip the light switch and realize
those are not "pearls" but teeth.

I feel around my mouth with my tongue.
Teeth feel loose,
gaps where there are none;
in those spaces are the grooves of my roots—
another tooth topples,
and I can feel it resting in the pocket
between my gums and jaw.
I spit it out—
blood,
panic,
heart
racing,
hands
shaking.

And then I wake.

All my teeth in place.

A recurring dream.
Nightmare.

Mr. Manicotti says
dreams
are our mind's way
of working through
all that we cannot
during the day.

A SHOT

Nightmares need tea
and a shot of whiskey—
the caramel water
warms my insides,
weakens my imagination,
welcomes rest.

Dad's advice.

I tiptoe up the stairs
like a ninja
averting creaks
so as not to stir the fam.

I bypass the noise
of the basement door
by leaving it ajar.

I shuffle into the kitchen
toward the cabinet above the fridge
only Dad and I can reach,
snag the bottle of Jack,
turn on the kettle
and watch so it doesn't whistle.
As I sip my tea I see
two shadows
on the tweed sofa
snuggled with a quilt.

It's Mom and Eve.

MANUAL: HOW TO TALK TO PARENTS

I wish there were a manual
for navigating awkward
conversations with parents.

On our way to pick up Brandy,
I want to talk to Mom about Eve.
I'm not sure where to begin.
I look at our parallel parking cartoon
and figure, *Let's give it a go.*

Drive around until you find a spot that looks big enough.
    I have about four blocks to say something.
Pull up even to the front car.
    I lean over to gauge Mom's mood. Exhausted.
Stop.
    I take a deep breath.
While stopped, turn your wheel all the way to the right.
    I noticed you've been spending a lot of time with Eve lately.
Turn around and look out the back of your car.
    I lean over to gauge Mom's mood. Still exhausted.
Begin backing up.
    It seems like she's a good friend for you.
Stop.
    "She is a great comfort to me. She knows what it's like."
Turn your wheel all the way to the left.
    What "what's" like?
Keep backing in facing the wheels forward.
      "Having a big family. Having a distant husband.
      Not having— good morning, Brandy."

A paper plate, wrapped in pink tinted cellophane
stretches between the driver and passenger's seats
perfectly parked between me and Mom.

"My dad and I made these to thank you.
Nigerian coconut candy.
Dad cracked the coconuts—
hmm, that must be why he calls me
coconut head—
but I grated the meat.
It's really easy—
coconut juice,
powdered sugar,
high heat,
caramelize, brown,
then cool to candy.
It's way better than anything at Ferrara.
Anyway, Dad says *thank you*—
and I do, too."

"Remember *Candy Girl*?"
I ask Brandy as I take a bite.
"Good times."

"Good times."

BRANDY'S MOM

Brandy's mom
left them
when we were in junior high,
left them
for another man,
for another life,
all White,
which is harsh, I know.
If she hadn't
left them
she'd be out an inheritance:
parents' racism.
If she hadn't
left them,
who would Brandy be?
Who will Brandy become?

SHOWERING

A baby crawls on the woolen rug
inches from the fireplace grate.
A young mother sweeps him up,
says, "He's everywhere these days."

"Here, open this one next.
It's from Eve," Mom says,
smiling with—
what's that—
pride?

A convertible stroller:
chrome accented black wheels,
plush fabric,
vegan leather,
all-terrain,
reversible seat,
flat recline,
transforms into a pram with bassinet
in a cinch.

That was a big wish
on the register list.
This baby is going to stroll in style.

"Looks like the baby has a nice new ride,
but how about somewhere to sleep?"
says Toni, standing.
"Come with us to the basement."

And there, in the corner of Hope's basement
stands a white, solid wood, craftsman-style crib.
Sheets striped with yellow, blue, green, and pink.
A musical mobile with photo clips.

"We all chipped in: Hannah, Faith, Sadie, me.
You can clip photos of us to the mobile,
program songs.
Listen.

"Bridge Over Troubled Water" plays softly.

A PRECEDENT

Hannah (#7) looks like me.
Rather I look like Hannah.
Unruly brown hair,
olive-toned skin
courtesy of our Italian genes—
only she's six inches shorter than me.
Natalia thinks I should use her ID
to buy beer
but I say: "What if the clerks look at the height?"

I've seen Hannah sorting,
offering more hand-me-downs,
just not jeans,
carting off books and trophies
to Goodwill,
throwing away old papers,
saving stuffed animals
for the new baby.

Aaron shows up Sunday night
in a suit with flowers for my mother
who's not home
and a book of poems for my father
who's always home.
Mary Oliver.
A poem bookmarked:
"The Summer Day."

Aaron and Dad
sit at the picnic table.
Hannah and I sit
at the top of the stairs,
holding hands,
eavesdropping.

He says, "Sir, I love your daughter,
who you have raised,
who I now love.
And I know you and Mary Oliver
appreciate a plan for our *one wild and precious life*,
so here's mine:
I'd like your blessing to live with your daughter;
now I know that is a sin,
but I think it is a responsible one
if we are to know, truly know,
we can share a life together.
So if after a year, we are still alive
and in love, I will come back to you and ask
for Hannah's hand in marriage."

Hannah and I look at
our hands
intertwined
then smile
into
each
other's
eyes.

Sisters.

WALKING IT OFF

Fluorescent lights paint
young faces younger,
old faces older.

Toni runs off the court
during warm ups
to hug Teresa and me,
to thank us for coming
to her volleyball game.

She looks so young—

almost as tall as
I was at her age
but with pale, freckled skin
like Teresa,
blue eyes like Dad,
definitely more athletic than
I was at her age.

Teachers look so old—

try to rub Teresa's belly,
offer her a seat,
but she wants to walk,
urge the baby to exit.

Toni plays great—

bowed ponytail flailing
as she jumps and dives.

In between cheers, we
feel stares,
hear whispers,
notice selfie-stances
in our direction
from the bleachers.

"F- them," says Teresa.
"I am carrying a human being.
They're just carrying cell phones."

I can't tell if Teresa looks
younger or older.

HONEY

"My three little girls, how was the game?
Did you spike the ball? Make some bumps, Toni?"
Mom says all full of cheer
like she didn't just miss another game,
like she didn't just go shopping with Eve,
like she didn't just buy sheets, towels,
and what else is in this Target bag?
Picture frames?

"Mom, it's called a *kill;*
it's called a *pass,*
and, yes, all that," Toni explains.
"But you missed it, again."

Mom pretends not to hear,
starts humming Dolly Parton.

"Mom, are these for me?" asks Teresa.

"No, honey. They're for me and…"

"Ma, we can't afford this.
Didn't you notice?
No electricity this morning," I say.

"Not to worry, honey.
Borrowed some money from Eve.
Stopped by ComEd today.
You'll be able
to dry all that hair—
don't know why you don't just
cut it all off."

Here we go again…

"Why is she so happy, *honey*?" I whisper to Toni,
sitting next to me in the back seat.

"In our S.O.S. lesson today,
I learned that people depressed
get a surge of happiness,
seem less stressed
when they decide to—" says Toni.

"Buy sheets and towels?"

And then I think:
What has Mom
decided for herself?

MARCH

IN LIKE A LION

In second grade,
Mrs. Mooney's March bulletin board
hosted a pride of lions near the first
and a flock of lambs near the end
to symbolize the moody Chicago month.

The Taurus is nearly blown over
by a gust of wind,
nearly washed from the road
by sideways rain
as my knuckles pale
at ten and two.
Henry's eyes close
in the rearview mirror,
meditating through the storm.

"Oh, Mr. M., we gotta go
to the hospital," Brandy whispers
to the side of his headrest.
"Just got a text.
I know. I know.
No cell phones, but
Teresa's having her baby."

"Sadie, take a left up ahead;
we're taking a little detour," Mr. Manicotti says.
"And stop with the deep breathing, Henry.
You're making me nervous."

I take us to the hospital room
where my fourteen-year-old sister,
legs in stirrups,
grasps the birthing bar,
white-knuckling through each contraction,
failing gloriously at those deep Lamaze breaths.

Dad tells us to go back to school,
"It could be a while."

Mom takes her hand,
"Don't worry, honey;
he'll come out when he's ready."

Fifteen hours later,
our pride is a cub bigger,
the wind has subsided,
and the rain rests in a drizzle.

A GLIMPSE

Even though Sam is not twenty-one,
he tells me to drive his car to the hospital
after work.

Behind-the-wheel hours with Sam.

He insists we stop at Jewel on the way
to buy a wildflower bouquet
because Teresa is no carnation.

We shuffle through the hospital hallway,
stammering words and pace,
lingering in the silence
of this boyfriend-ish moment
until
I hear the cries
of a baby confused about his new world;
I hear the panic
of my sister pleading with her newborn son;
I hear the words
of a mother
teaching her daughter how to breastfeed,
shushing an incompetent nurse,
ordering her friend to position a pillow.

Bouquet trembling,
heart quavering,
I peek into the room
to see a familiar chaos
so many siblings escaped before me,

and I understand
why
my mother doesn't want to do *this*
again.

I want to take the baby and soothe his cries.
I want to tell my mom that she's done enough.
I want to tell my sister that everything will be okay.
I want to ask this woman if she is my mom's lover.

But instead,
I turn to leave,
bump into Sam
hand the bouquet to the incompetent nurse,
re-wrap my scarf,
clutch the car keys,
and drive us home in silence.

I put the car in park.
I feel Sam reach for me.
His palm holds my cheek
as I turn towards him.
His eyes hold my gaze,
as mine wet.
His lips taste my tears,
then find mine
parted to welcome
his comfort.

GRILLED CHEESE

The porch light is illuminated
by someone
watching,
waiting
with a stuffed elephant.

I put my hand over Sam's,
close my eyes
to swim in this moment a bit longer,
then reach for the unlock button.

"Wait," Sam says.
"You don't want me to come in?"

"It's Toni," I say.
"Home alone.
Mom and Dad likely forgot
about her.
She's only
twelve years old.
Probably
just eating dry cereal
alone."

"I'll make her something—
us—
something."

Sam makes us grilled cheese.
Brings it to me and Toni

quilted-up on the sofa
watching Wonder Woman cartoons.
Toni offers Sam
a corner of our quilt.

"Time for bed," I say to Toni, hoping for some Sam time.

"Carry me?" she pleads, holding up her arms to him.

Sam carries Toni upstairs.
I follow.
She sinks into his arms,
burrows her face in his shoulder.
When was the last time I hugged Toni?
When was the last time anyone hugged Toni?

Sam can't rest Toni on her bed.
She sleeps on the floor—
same way I did before
my chamber in the basement.

He rolls out her blanket,
fluffs her pillow,
tucks her in,
offers a fist bump—
no judgment
in his patient, blue eyes.

As we descend the stairs, I try to explain:
"Four or five to a room...
 no space for beds or bunks...
side-by-side...
a row of caterpillars wiggling for space...
whispering stories and wishes."

"Do I smell grilled cheese?"
Dad calls from downstairs.

I look at Sam and say,
"Will you make one more?"

PIGGY BACK RIDES FOR BATHS

Kids, it's time for baths.
>> Hop on my back.
>>> Hup, two, three, four.
Line up at the stairs.
>> Your turn. Hop on.
>>> Hup, two, three, four.
The water is almost ready.
>> Next. Hop on.
>>> Hup, two, three, four.
>>> Do you want three or four or more?
My, all so big.
Just three.
Hop in.
Lather the soap.
Wash each other's backs.
Be gentle.
Stand.
Run the water.
Grab a cup.
Rinse off your sisters' suds.
Let's go snow monkeys,
soaking in the hot springs.
Time to get out.
Towel off.
One. Squeeze.
Two. I love you.
Three. Oh, Sadie.
Three more, please.

Bath time perfected.

FRENCH

I don't quite know what to make of that kiss.
I've been kissed before.
There was that boy in fourth grade, Shane.
I'm pretty sure he tripped me so he'd have to kiss my knee.
Then there was that boy in sixth, Denny.
On the lips, but that's it: four lips touching
for like six
seconds.
There were a few more kisses like that
until freshman year.

Dean.
He introduced me to french kissing,
lower case because it wasn't that romantic
with
him.
With him, kissing was a means to an end.
french kissing
      meant hands could move
          over-the-shirt,
              under-the-shirt,
                  over the jeans,
                      which meant, well,
it meant nothing
to
me.

Once, I was in Dean's room
and noticed on his Chicago Bears calendar
my name with a line extending for a few days.
I flipped back a few months,
and there it was again and again.
He was charting my periods.
He actually thought he could—
that I would—
such
a
jerk.

But with Sam,
I am going to admit,
that
was
my
first
real
kiss.
French.

DOUBLE SHIFTS

Nelly and Natalia
go to the Dells for spring break.
I stay home to
work
double
shifts.

Double shifts.
The lunch rush ends around one, maybe two.
The dinner rush starts around four, maybe five.

Sam removes his sauce-stained apron
and bandana and pulls his
hair-tie from his smooth, blond locks,
says, "I am going home between shifts. Want to come?"

Opening my Psych book,
averting my eyes,
pulling on my bun
to release my tresses,
to tease just a little,
I say, "Where's home?"
thinking, *No, thanks. It's been too many
days since that kiss. Why do girls have to
wait around for guys to decide.*

"I got a place in Hillside, a few miles away.
Nothing special. We can chill. Watch a movie.
Talk.
About us.
Just not here.
Luigi's too nosy."

Sam stacks my books and watches as
I pull at my messy, messier bun,
my unruly tresses knotted in elastic.
My cheeks flush, my heart races—
some tease.

"Stop fussing. Let me." With his teeth
he breaks the band. "You're free. Let's go."

And I do.
Hoping he doesn't have piles of dirty dishes.
Hoping he doesn't have little hairs on his soap.
Hoping he says he wants to kiss me again.

SAM'S PLACE

Kitchen is pristine—
labels face the same way.

Living room is cozy—
worn leather sofa, floral recliner.

Bedroom is boyish—
plaid comforter, sports posters.

"I'm going to shower," he says.
"Here's a t-shirt and shorts.
You can take a nap.
I bet my bed is more
comfortable than the floor—
no offense."

He closes the bathroom door.
A full length mirror faces me.
I watch as I
untie my apron,
pull off Luigi's tee,
peel away my black work jeans,
and see
my body.
Cowlicks and curls,
dress my shoulders.
I feel beautiful
in this space
beyond my home.

Sam hums
in the shower.

I smile
in the mirror
and watch
Sam's shirt,
Sam's shorts,
Sam's bed,
welcome my
body.

In seconds,
I am asleep,
wrapped in
Cubs and Bears.

WAKING

When I wake,
Sam is
watching me,
lying beside me,
reaching for me.

He smells of Irish Spring.
His hair is damp.
He is wrapped in Hawks and Bulls.

"So you must really like Chicago sports, huh?" I say.

"You. Are. Beautiful." he says
pulling me into his chest.

"In *your* clothes?" I ask.

"In *my* clothes,
(kiss) in an apron,
(kiss) in a parka,
(kiss) in a frown,
(kiss) in a tear,
(kiss) in a smile,
(kiss) in my hands."

I feel how his hands move me
to breathe more deeply.
I feel how I can move him
by pressing my hips against his.

And I love that our feet are hanging off the bed.

And then Sam rolls over.
"Sadie, you drive me crazy."

I pull at his arm, but he shakes me off,
throws his legs to the side,
sits elbows on knees.
"You should get dressed. It's time."

I pull off the Cubs shirt,
toss it on the bed,
linger in my bra
to see if he'll take a peek.
He does, but says,
"Don't."

SECOND SHIFT

No awkward silence.
Sam sings in the car—
every word to
every song.

As we clock in,
Luigi gives me a wink,
says I have a couple,
early birds waiting.
Table nineteen.

I tie on my apron,
a few sauce stains from lunch,
knot my hair in a bun— no tie,
march over to nineteen
and say, "Hi,
my name is—"

And there sits my
6' 6" Santa
with his wife.

CHRISTMAS IN MARCH

Oh. My. God.
Ever notice how Shame is never far away?
Six months dormant,
the consciousness
of my disgrace
arises swiftly,
painfully.

"Of course, Sam's Sadie.
You are lovely, just as Sam said.
And so hardworking and smart.
Your parents must be so proud,"
Mrs. Claus says.

"Sam says," Santa leans in, voice softening,
"Sam says, someday, he's going to marry you."

Santa leans back.
Runs his hands over his silver slicked back hair.
Smoothes his beard.
Surveys my face.
Smiles.

"But—
he needs to be who he's going to be.
And—
you need to be who you are going to be.
Apart.
Before.
Together.
Plus, he's an adult, and you're still—
well, not legal,"
Santa giggles, rosy-cheeks glistening.

"Hon, that was private.
The shot you did with Luigi
must be going to your head
and lips,"
Mrs. Claus says.
"Pay him no mind, dear.
He's just saying…well,
Sam is fond of you."

Stunned—
I stand as Embarrassment and Rejection
tangle with Shame in my belly.

"Wow, Sam's parents, huh?" I manage to murmur.
"I'll, um, tell Sam you're here."

"Tell him you have some *tough* customers," says Santa,
blues eyes twinkling. "We want to surprise him."

The best I can do is nod
as I take a step toward
the kitchen
thinking
Sam has said more about *me than* to *me.*
thinking
This must be why he wanted me to come over.
thinking
This is why I don't lean, *Mr. Manicotti.*

"Oh, and Sadie," Santa calls.
"Glad you seem to be
making better choices."

I blink away a drop of Shame.

Some Christmas in March.

LECTURE

As I count my Washingtons, Lincolns, and Hamiltons to deposit,
Sam wants to talk, to explain all the info his parents dropped.
He tells me he has dreams of
us
together—
one day—
after we've both had a chance
to become ourselves
by ourselves
beyond
our families.

He tells me I have to grow, go to college, live on my own.
He tells me I have to travel the world.
He tells me I have to find Sadie beyond the Carters.

He tells me he has to find his place, his purpose—
school is not his thing.
He tells me he has a chance to become a police officer,
says he's what they need these days: decency on the force.
He tells me he is finding Sam beyond the Mohers,
knows who he can be, likes what he sees.

I do, too.

But who will I be, become?
If I leave to find me, I may never come back.

And then the bell on the front door chimes.
"We're closed," I call.

It's Henry Lucas.

"Dad and I were
logging some hours behind the wheel.
I wondered if you'd…
I mean if we could…
I mean if you're not busy… "
Henry stops.
Looks at me.
Looks at Sam.
Sees.

"Oh, sorry…
did I interrupt
something?"

"Naw, man, I am Sam,"
reaching out his hand.
"Sadie's—
I was just leaving."

"Henry. Nice to meet you, Sam."

And then Henry and Sam shake hands.
And then Sam walks into the kitchen.
And then Henry asks me out.

A LAMB AND A LIBRARY

In like a lion.
The storms that welcomed March
have subsided.

Out like a lamb.
The sun warms my hoodie
on my two-mile walk—
forty minutes of
sun-kissed reverie
accompanied by
singing robins
and wind whispers.

Henry's waiting for me
at the library
when I arrive.
He offers
a smile,
a coffee,   .
a donut,
and a backpack of books.

A sheep
in its first year
is called a lamb,
which symbolizes
renewal,
tenderness,
gentleness, and
innocence—

also the perfect victim
for sacrifice.

What will this
beginning
with Henry
bring?

BENCH QUESTIONS

Do you drink coffee?   *At work, sometimes.*

Do you like glazed or sprinkled?   *Glazed.*

Do you still read?   *Not much.*

Why not?   *The conch shell.*

     Lord of the Flies.

     The green light.

     The Great Gatsby.

     The crucifix.

     The Stranger.

Ah, SparkNotes.   *It's all analysis.*

     No getting lost in another world.

     No getting to know people I will never meet.

     I know it sounds lame,

     But that's why I read, read (past tense).

     Why my ice cream always

melted.   *Yeah, sorry about that.*

Donuts

don't

melt.

OPENING DOORS

We're the first ones to arrive
as the doors slide aside
and Marge welcomes Henry
with a suspicious glare for me.

"Oh, I think she's sweet on you," I whisper.

"She's my lady, Sadie," Henry says.
"And the best librarian in the `burbs."

"We have it all ready for you, Henry.
A shelf just with
selections from 305.4,
a few memoirs, too."

"Thanks, Marge.
Here's a donut for later.
Sprinkles, your fav," he whispers, winks.

"Who is with your mom?" I whisper.

"Yoga class in our living room,
but she's getting out more
and more these days.
Meditation."

I nearly fall over when I see
For Henry Lucas.
A stack of books.
The spines, a poem for me:

Freedom is a Constant Struggle
Between Two Worlds
We Should All Be Feminists
Daring to Drive
The Unfinished Revolution

*Angela Davis, Zainab Salbi, Chimamanda Ngozi Adichie, Manal Sharif, Minky Worden

UNVEILING

Something comes over me or off me—
an unveiling of sorts.
I am overcome or coming undone,
dropping to my knees
to see and hold these books,
to read the words of these worlds,
to bear witness to lives beyond my own.

Henry lowers, kneels beside me
with a knowing smile,
kisses my cheek and points me to a seat—
a big leather chair
by the window
overlooking
a garden waiting to become
wildflowers.

I read Adichie.

She says we teach girls shame.
She says girls grow into women
who silence themselves.
She says we should all be angry.
She says we must do better.

For 64 pages,
I am not lost.
I do not escape,
do not feel flutters,
do not feel quivers,

just a flow
of thought about
my life,
hers,
our places in this world.

I want to drink coffee with Adichie in Nigeria,
or at least stay in this chair for the next year,
but I have to prep lettuce for antipasti salads,
so I close the book and hold it to my heart.

"Same time, same place tomorrow?"
Henry asks
but knows.

Yes, thank you.

WAITING

When I get off work,
Henry is waiting for me
in the parking lot,
sitting on his bicycle,
adjusting his knit beanie
with one hand,
holding an apple
with the other.

"Thought I'd walk you home
unless you'd like to try a ride?"
he says, raising one eyebrow.

And before I can speak,
a car pulls up,
a window lowers,
"Is Sam still here?"
Anti-Valentines Miranda.

And before I can speak,
Sam is getting into the passenger seat.

"See ya, Sadie," says Anti-Valentines Miranda.

Sam waves as she closes the window.

"So how about that ride?" asks Henry.

THANK YOU

I opt out of Henry's offer
to pedal me home,
but I accept the melting
ice cream sandwich and walk
alongside Henry and his bike
in silence.

When we get to
my driveway,
Henry leans his bicycle
against the street lamp,
adjusts his knit beanie,
and says, "Sadie?"

"Yes, Henry?"

"What were you thinking about
on our walk? You know, you get
this crease in between your eyebrow
folds holding your thoughts
hostage."

I was thinking about Sam—
how he chiseled away at my wall,
how it felt good to let him,
how I really liked the touch,
how my fingers are sticky.

"I was thinking," I say,
"it was so sweet of you

to walk me home,
to bring me ice cream.
And…"

I reach for Henry's hands,
slide my fingers between his,
bring our hands
to my heart,
smile at our shadow
dancing on the driveway
and say, "Thank you."

Henry almost goes in for a kiss,
but he resists,
saddles his bike and says,
"Since sixth grade, Sadie,
I've wanted you,
to take care of you.
Let me."

Henry opens the wet wipes pouch,
gently cleanses my sticky palms,
then kisses my hands
one at a time
before riding off
in the moonlight.

My hands smell of lemons,
but the *take care of you*
is what lingers.

APRIL

JUST NO

"Need some help with that?" I hear.

"No, thanks, just a lapse in memory—
spring break," I say trying to get my locker open.

"I have it memorized: 19-29-9.
Funny, all those nines, like your birth order, huh?"

I turn around to see Dean—
bigger than ever and with acne.
Must be the roids. Gross.

Dean leans against my locker.

"Did you hear? Broke up with Natalia.
She's so immature with her room swap idea.
Me and Donnie bailed.
Spent the break lifting."

"Too bad. For some reason, she really liked you,"
I say, hugging my new books from Henry.

"You know. We were pretty good together.
Since things have changed in your family, maybe…
you know…"

"Hell. No."

Locker. Slam.

MY EDUCATION

I decide I will make my study hall
a second English class
slash first History class, which
isn't even a required course.

I decide I will borrow books
from Henry's shelf,
ask Marge for my own shelf,
make a note to bring her
donuts with sprinkles to win her over
even though I suspect
what she loves are
Henry's dimples.

After my introduction to feminism by Adichie,

I meet Manal Sharif, a Saudi woman,
    ...it took me a long time to break the chains inside me.

                  I meet Zainab Salbi, an Iraqi woman,
                     ...how casually we treat casualties.

        I meet Loung Ung, a Cambodian woman,
      ...the chance to do something that's worth me being alive.

I meet Wangari Maathai, a Kenyan woman,
    ...you are a gift to your communities and indeed the world.

These women say—

>*This is my story.*
>>*I am that girl.*
>>>*I have lived this.*

I open the journal
I started with Mr. M.
and
begin
to
write
my
story.

FATHERING

Dad spends most of his days at Hope's
helping Teresa with the baby.
Teresa says he is really sweet
with the little one—
swaddling,
bottling,
diapering,
bathing—
that all she wants to do is
sleep.

Dad tells me our new
mother Teresa
has postpartum
depression:
can't handle it

                                           feels guilty

            baby deserves better

                                                            emptiness

                                    numbness

disconnected.

I have disconnected,
avoiding the new mom and babe.
I am holding back,
withholding some piece of me.

At work,
Sam asks me how I can be so selfish.
He's the only child after all.
Aren't big families all about helping one another?
But I don't help.
I spend more time at work.
I spend more time at the library.
I spend more time with Henry.

I can't stop thinking about what Teresa
said that first day of school: "When will you
stand
up
for
me?"

And for me?
Who will
stand
up
for
me?

MEDITATING

I can walk to Henry's house
from school.
Walking is like praying,
a bridge between panic and peace.

Mrs. Lucas is beautiful.
Blonde, tall, lean—
a blonde version of me.
She pours two glasses of water
infused with cucumber and lavender,
hands them to Henry.
She plates a bunch of red grapes,
makes sure I know they're organic,
hands them to me.

"Take these upstairs,"
she says closing herself into
her yoga studio.

"Meditation," Henry whispers.
"She's much better these days.
Come on. I'll show you my room."

When I don't move,
he does,
linking his finger in my belt loop,
pulling me toward him,
pausing to question my eyes,
to brush his bangs from his,
to tuck my whispies behind my ear,

to wet his lips,
to wait for mine.

I exhale lavender and ask for more
with each step
toward his room,
closer to him.

I am so hungry,
but I want to savor
every second,
every taste.

I can't get over the ripples in his stomach,
the strength of his arms
hovering him above me
between kisses,
but what is more beautiful
is his weight pressed upon
my chest,
my breasts compressed,
hearts reaching through layers of flesh,
flurrying beats that can't quite reach
each other
as hard as we try,
and we try
until

I am full.

HOMECOMING

High chair at the picnic table.
Bottles piled up in the kitchen sink.
Pile of socks and onesies folded perfectly
on the stairs.
Swaddled baby in Dad's arms.
Teresa sleeping on the worn tweed sofa,
holding Ellie, the beloved elephant.

SELF-PRESERVATION

Mom refuses to be silent.
"How dare you bring them here?" she screams.
"How dare you go behind my back.
We agreed.
What about *us*?
What about *our* marriage?
We agreed."

Dad remains silent.

Mom is using her voice.
I can hear her anger,
and it is painfully beautiful.

"You. You. Hiding out
with that, that canoe
while I work two jobs,
clean this house,
do the laundry,
shop for food,
beg, borrow, and steal
to keep our lights on.
This, this— was not the plan."

Dad uses his fist.
Pounds on the picnic table.
Says in a whisper-shout,
"Enough. This is not about you.
And don't pretend
you want an *us*.

This is about the child—
our child who needs
help to become
a mother this little one
deserves.

She. They
are
our
us."

"I can't be part of your *our*," Mom says
with a tone I've never heard before,
an unwavering declaration.

And I wonder if this is what
Audre Lorde meant
when she said:
Caring for myself is not self-indulgence;
it is self-preservation, and
that is an act of political warfare.

And I see my mother
stride to the coat closet,
roll out a pre-packed duffle,
hoist the sack of towels and sheets,
drape a beige trench coat over her arm,
and leave
Lilac Lane.

Eve is waiting for her in the driveway.

DRIVING DESTINY

Faith is ambivalent.
On one hand,
she has Mom's car.
On the other hand,
she has to drive
me and Brandy
to zero hour.

We don't talk much.
Faith is on a mission
to graduate first in her class,
to move across the country
for an education
beyond the Midwest,
beyond the Carters,
and to do it all
on
her
own.

I look at Faith's hands at ten and two,
driving in my mother's seat,
also daring to imagine a way of being for
her
self.

Manal al-Sharif says that
it's not about driving a car;
it's about being in the driver's seat
of
our
destiny.

And I wonder
where I will drive
when
I
have
the
seat.
Will
I
leave?

FLUTTERS OF FAMILY

All my life,
I have followed the rhythms of our family,
finding my place in line,
walking in the footprints
ahead of mine.
Still, there was only
the appearance of order
as we sat side-by-side in the
church pew,
as we waited in the corner
at the hardware store,
as we were carried
up the stairs for
communal baths.

The rhythms of chaos.

Still, as crazy as it was,
the discord was all we knew.

Our home—

the place where we made
a symphony of our spoons and cereal bowls,
a choir of S&G's "Bridge Over Troubled Water" out of key,
a sock-matching assembly line,
a constellation of stars
waiting to catch dreams.

The place where
one by one
each escapes
because
dreams are not realized here.

BABY DUTY

We take shifts babysitting Teresa
and the baby.

Hope works as a nurse,
stops by in the morning
after her shift,
brings diapers,
lots of wet wipes,
shows us how to keep the baby's
circumcision and umbilical
cord clean.

Aaron is in culinary school,
classes and job at night,
helps Dad most days,
brings groceries.
The first time the fridge
has seen fresh greens.
The first time Dad's
tasted cured meats.

Teresa says Aaron is a natural,
distracts Dad from the canoe,
makes everyone laugh—
medicine for their depression.

Faith is so smart and focused.
She's monitoring Teresa's
homework because
"a GED is not the same as
a high school diploma" and
"that baby deserves a
smart mom."

Hannah, Toni, and I
alternate books and bath time
in the same sink
Mom washed
our hair.

NEW COOK

"Order up," I say.

And then I see.

"Where's Sam?" I ask.

"Nice to meet you, too," he says,
walking back to his balls of dough.

"Don't mind the new guy," Barb says.

"Where's Sam?" I stammer feeling flutters.

"Honey, slow down. Relax.
He's fine. He started the academy.
They wanted him to have a degree,
but his dad pulled some strings," Barb says.
"We'll all miss him around here, huh?"

No more breakfast calabrese.
No more grapefruit juice for two.
No more life lectures.
No more kisses.
But that was his plan.

"Hey, your sister's here
to pick up a pizza," Barb says,
interrupting my pity party.

"Which one?"

ACCEPTANCE

It's Hope.

"Hey, Bean," she says,
the only one who calls me that.
"How much?"

"Luigi says it's on the house," I say.

"Yeah? He's always been good to me.
You know, I met Maggie here.
Luigi knew about us way before Mom and Dad.
He let us hang out after work, talk.
I didn't want to hide it from you guys,
but you know…the whole Catholic thing.
I guess I didn't want to be…"

"Rejected," I say.

"Right, I love her.
I just wanted to be with her,
be happy.
But I *did* miss you
when they kicked me out.
And I *was* mad—
hurt, angry, disgusted, rejected.
But nobody knows what it's like—
being in a big family,
the craziness of it all.
It's part of me.
I missed it.

Then Dad invited
us to Thanksgiving.
Us.
He wanted us
to take the baby,
thought maybe
Mom wouldn't leave.
But Mom left long ago,
and Teresa needs
all of us now,
and Dad needs
all of us now."

"Why doesn't *Mom* need us?
Why doesn't Mom *want* us?" I plead.

 "Eve left her husband, too.
It looks like Mom and Eve
had been planning
for some time
to start a new life
together.
Eve has money,
can offer Mom
security—
can offer Mom
understanding—
can offer Mom
affection, attention.
They're starting over."

"So they are … ?"

"Let's sit and eat this pizza.
Is booth nineteen open?"

BAPTISM

What happens to the souls
of children not baptized?
If we're born with sin,
and baptism is supposed
to cleanse us of that sin,
and I can't cleanse
my baby, will my baby go to Hell?

Teresa is rambling,
her depression
turned to anxiety.

At mass on Sunday,
I talk to Father O'Neill
who says,
Teresa should return to church
on her own first,
show her commitment
to raise the child in the Faith,
go to confession,
ask for forgiveness for her sin,
volunteer in clothing drives
and donut socials to show
she will serve God,
and abstain from future
pre-marital sex.

Teresa's not sure about the last part.

In a private ceremony,
no mention in the church bulletin,
Brandy becomes Godmother.
Aaron becomes Godfather.
Antonio
is
baptized.

When we get home,
soaking up the sun
on the front porch,
a Styrofoam cup
packed with dirt
a tiny green
leaf breaking
through,
greets us.

MAY

BIRTHDAY

Just one present.
Mom would say.
Keep it under twenty.
Here's some money.
Get one of your sisters to wrap it.
I'll put it next to your cereal bowl
on the big day.

Surprise!

The best present
was my very own
hair dryer.
I no longer had to wait
in line.

ONE-SIX

This year,
it's the big one-six.
I know there's no present;
everyone's been a little
distracted.

Plus,
Mom's the one
who remembered,
made everyone gather
for my cake of choice:
Sara Lee's original cream
cheesecake,
gooey strawberry topping.

As I amble up the basement stairs,
Faith's waiting with
Dad, Hope, Hannah,
Aaron, Teresa holding Antonio,
Toni holding Sara Lee's cheesecake
with a one
and a six
lit.

They stand for,
they sing to
me.

OBSTACLES

Mr. Manicotti makes arrangements
for just the two of us
to drive to the DMV
at nine,
to miss class
for this
final
exam.
Divine.

The parking lot
is
an obstacle course,
and I three-point turn,
throw it in reverse,
parallel and bay park
between cones,
around paper pedestrians,
accelerating,
breaking,
signaling.

"Pass."

WHEELS

Mr. Manicotti makes me an offer
to buy his beloved car
for $2000—
worth five—
because he heard me go on and on
all winter about
how much it means to me to be
able to drive to work,
able to help out at home,
able to leave if I need.

Mr. Manicotti makes me an offer
to study abroad
for $2000—
"priceless"—
because he heard me go on and on
all spring about
books, people, places
on the page.

A summer in Nepal.
A cultural exchange
of,
by,
for
girls
from around the world.

He hands me
a brochure with a bridge,
a form for a passport.

"Apply," he says.
"There's still time."

SISTAS' GIFTS

Confetti spills out of my locker.
Nelly, Natalia, and Brandy
are peeking around the
painted-too-many-times
blue-ish locker door,
looking guilty but cute.

They sing to me.

"Look inside," Brandy says,
reaching into my locker to reveal.

"Apparently, you have become
this feminist-activist-literary critic
while we've been chasing boys,"
 Nelly says.

"Books are safer than roided-idiots," says Natalia.

"Notice the spine poetry?" Brandy points proudly.

> *Between the World and Me*
> *I Shall Not Hate*
> *Never Fall Down*
> *A Time to Dance*
> *Sister Citizen*

"I notice, Brandy. I notice."

*Ta-Nehisi Coates, Izzeldin Abuelaish, Patricia McCormick, Padma Venkatraman, Claudia Rankine

LIGHTS

There must be a thousand
white, twinkle lights
draped in parallel
strings above our heads.
Christmas in May
on the patio of an
empty restaurant.

"Where are we?" I say,
untying my blindfold.

Henry shrugs his shoulders,
lays down his keys,
got his license before me,
says, "My favorite Italian restaurant;
they're usually closed on Mondays,
but it's your birthday
and my dad's a really good customer."

"Good evening, Miss Carter.
May I bring you some sparkling water?"

I pause.

Thinking of my mother, Mrs. Carter,
who would have loved for Dad
to do something like this
for
her.

"Sadie? You okay? Is this too much?"

"Yes. No. I mean, it's beautiful. Thank you."

"I just wanted to do something special
for
you."

We toast our sparkling water.

Henry sings
to
me.

SATIATED

Extra virgin olive oil,
fresh grated parmesan cheese,
warm, rustic bread
for dipping.

Linguini with clams
basted in lemon juice,
a scene from
Lady and the Tramp
unraveling.

Ladyfingers soaked in cognac,
layers of mascarpone cheese,
espresso, cocoa powder:
tiramisu.

We hold hands across the table
between bites.
We talk about books
and the lights.
When he drops his napkin,
he stands to kiss
the cocoa powder
from
my
lips.

Then, there's a gift
with
an ice cream sandwich.

HIS GIFT

Pink paper
no bow
but
a
note:
Meet me there.

Inside the box is
a plane ticket.

Hear me out:
Next month,
we're leaving for Bali.
Mom's been getting better,
you know.
Meditation has really
helped.
Dad's taking us on a family trip.
Yoga on the beach.
Long walks in silence.
Exotic fruits.
Sunshine.

I
want you to meet us there,
want to be my Higher Self with you,
want you to take care of you.

You said you wanted
  to see a world beyond the Carters.
This can be the beginning.
Our beginning.
Let me show you
a real
family.

A PRAYER

The panic
is even in the rain;
it itches my umbrella

like a scab wanting to,
be picked,
taunting me to resist,
as I walk to church

to do the only
thing I know that
bridges the panic
and the peace.

Pray.

Only when I get to church,
the rain has stopped.
I don't feel the need to
go
in.
I've prayed
all
along
the
way.

I know what I must do.

I know what's *real*.

BEACH BLINK

I sit beside an
enormous dune,
created by wind
I can't see
and white-capped waves
that push and pull,
steps away
from Godmother's place
in the early morning
writing this moment
and the next
on the left
of the page
phrases and fragments
that are mine
protecting the white
on the right—
space for stories that are not
mine
to
tell.

The page—
always partial
yet
somehow
enough.

"*Très chic*, birthday girl,"
she says, snapping a pic.

Sitting beside me,
she shows me my
image before
removing from her pack
a thermos of hot coffee,
a freshly baked blueberry scone.
I
see on the screen
a mane of long, wild waves
braided with tassels
from the scarf,
sun-shimmering cheeks
in pink,
a face I haven't seen—
of course,
I blinked.

"Eat," she says,
handing half a scone.

I savor every crumb
of butter and blueberry,
lick the sugar granules
from my palm.

"Have you decided,
my dear Goddaughter,
what you will do this summer?"

"Yes, I have."

She stands,
does not ask,

does not advise,
brushes sand from her backside,
bends to look me in the eyes,
hands on my cheeks,
a kiss on my forehead,
a knowing smile.

I love that
she
sees
Me.

JUNE

VALEDICTORIAN

My name is Faith Carter,
and I have plans— big plans.
Tell me, what is it you plan to do with your one wild and precious life?
What have you done with it thus far?
I'll tell you how I've spent mine.

Working.

Baking delicious chocolate croissants at four bucks a pop.
And, yes, I know how to correctly pronounce croissants in French
because I took two years of it in junior high and four years of it here,
but I've never been anywhere I had to actually say it like this: croissant.

Throwing pitches into a net nine months out of the year
to play varsity softball only to have a bum shoulder and no scholarship.

Captaining a volleyball team the other three months,
oozing team spirit, racking up records, bruising my hips, and for what?

Studying ACT and SAT test prep books for fun, borrowed and returned
from the library so many times but never with a fine, my proudest
accomplishment.

But really this.

This.

This is my proudest accomplishment.

This moment when I ask:
What is it you plan to do with your one wild and precious life?

And this moment when I answer:
My plan is to have some fun.

PARTY

"Faith! Faith, congrats. Can't wait for you to join me in Arizona,"
says #2.

> "For real, Faith. Awesome,"
> says #4.

"I thought you'd give some lecture about ambition,"
says #5.

> "Dope. Too bad Mom didn't hear,"
> says #6.

"I think she's in Italy with Eve,"
says #1.

"Thanks for that," I say
glaring at #s 6 and 1.
"Let's get some cake, Faith."

"Thanks for the save,
but I do wish she—"

"Cake. We need cake!"

Arm in arm,
we stroll
to the table,
cloth blowing in the wind,
cake knife reflecting the sun,
drops of water from the pool
sprinkled on the hem.

Then a shadow
drifts and I hear,

"Can I help you with that?
Scratch that. You clearly need help."

It's Sam,
holding Antonio.

"Hope you don't mind
I crashed your party, Faith.
Aaron thought I could
help…uh…
with the food,
but Antonio was crying, so…"

"Well, he's smiling now," I say.

"I'll…um…check on Dad," says Faith.

I reach for Antonio, for the first time.
Snuggling him in my arms, for the first time.

"Are you happy, little one?" I say.

"Are you?" asks Sam.
"I really just came to see…
I mean…are you?
Sadie?
Are you happy?"

"Happy?"

"Hey, Sam. Give me a hand,"
Aaron shouts across the pool.

And Sam leaves me to swoon
over my nephew.

Happy.

GOING-AWAY GIVING

In my corner bedroom,
I set aside my four-inch foam mattress,
push up the makeshift frame,
make space to pack my duffle.
Days will be hot, humid.
Nights will be cool, breezy:
brother's jeans,
sister's Keds,
faded hoodie,
new sundress and flip flops,
a week of underwear,
will do laundry there.

I don't bring anything to control my hair.
I will let the cowlicks and curls go awry.
Just a carry-on for me.
I learned checked bags are
pricey.

Then I pack four envelopes
that will stay behind.

For Dad:
rent for the month I'm gone,
registration and fee for summer volleyball camp,
a note for Coach— *I'll miss the first week,*
but I'll work on my timing and teaming— and
an application for Dad to reinstate his teaching license with fee.

For Brandy:
my Adichie,
my Lorde,
and a book of poems by Angelou,
I marked, "Still I Rise."

For Toni:
my infinity scarf,
to replace Ellie,
Antonio's
beloved object.

For Teresa:
a letter.

DEAR TERESA,

Mr. Manicotti will babysit anytime.
Call him. Let him help you.
Make time for Toni.
Eat ice cream and hug her, a lot.
Make sure there's always food in the house.
Here's some cash for Aldi,
just save me a Pop-Tart
for when I return.

And Teresa,
I'm sorry for all the times
I did not stand up for you.
My legs are becoming stronger.
I'll do and be better.

And Teresa,
you're going to be okay;
Antonio will show you the way.

Peace,
Sadie

TERMINAL

Hannah,
my big sister—
not my mom,
not my dad—
takes me
to the airport.

O'Hare.
International terminal.
Departures.

Hannah
does her best
to mother me:

"Toothbrush?
Tampons?
Tylenol?"

"Check. Check. Check.
Isn't it a little late
to ask me this?"

"Right. Right.
Passport?
Boarding pass?
Camera?"

"Check. Check. No."

Hannah hands me
an I-Phone 4S,
says the camera still works.
Hannah hands me
a twenty,
says just in case.
Hannah hugs me,
says I'll be fine,
says
we
will
be
fine.

SECURITY

Security beckons me
to stand arms over head,
barefoot, bare shouldered,
a stance of surrender.

I walk in my mind through the year
that brought me to this place,
this chamber
where I wait.

Santa's eyes, Thanksgiving pies,
Luigi's pizzas, Manicotti's lectures,
Mom's departure, Antonio's arrival,
Sam's tree, Henry's library.

"Please, step out, ma'am.
Ma'am?"

My cheeks flushed.
My heart pounds.
My vision halo-s in white light.

Will Dad step up?
Will Mom come back?
Will Teresa love Antonio?
Will he love me?
Am I happy?
Maybe I should have just bought a car.

"Ma'am! You can put your arms down now."

BRIDGES

I stand at the bridge with my
pack on my back,
ready to start
my study abroad.

A crew of girls
and chaperones
have gone ahead.

I hear laughter
on the other side.
I see flashes of
red capes
catching the air.

The bus driver
holds his hands in prayer,
nods,
urges me to go on
with his eyes.

I cross the bridge
to see
my sisters,
my teachers,
my students:
Buddhist nuns
in their saffron robes
with beautiful bare heads
playing volleyball.

One nun
sitting on the sidelines
greets me, hands to heart,
eyes flutter
with my curls
blowing in the wind.

And I see
in her dark, brown eyes
my mother—
a teenage girl
who joined the convent
to escape her father's disdain,
to become a self
free from his gaze
until she was ready
to make a family of her own.

In this school
women learn
to build bridges
from east to west,
becoming teachers
in the service of peace.
I will help my sisters
with English,
and they will help me
with being,
with becoming
until summer's gone.

Our liberation
is bound up
with
one
another,
says Lilla Watson.

And so it is.

ALONE TOGETHER

Alone,
I have to live
with my choices;
I have to endure
the whispers of self-doubt I create;
I have to assuage
the flutters and quivers;
I have to build
the bridge between panic and peace.
Only together
can I understand
what it means to be
my parents' daughter,
my siblings' sister,
a friend,
a citizen
to and in
this world,
who lives within and beyond our choices
alone together.

When I return home,
I will not have a car,
but I know
my strong legs
will take me
where I need to be.

AUTHOR'S NOTE

I wrote *Alone Together* in verse because I see the stanzas and line breaks as representing Sadie's fragmented thinking and limited perspective on the complexity of her family and purpose in life.

Like Sadie, I grew up in a big family. I can't possibly know what it was like to be the oldest with so many younger siblings or to be the youngest with so many older siblings, so the white spaces on the page are for their stories. And the white spaces on these pages are for the verses of *your* life. I hope that you write them.

Maslow's hierarchy of needs helped me tell Sadie's story. In his 1943 paper titled "A Theory of Human Motivation," Abraham Maslow describes stages he believed necessary for human subsistence and fulfillment. Many people understand this to mean that in order to reach the higher stages like self-actualization, you must have your more basic needs satisfied, such as security, but I wanted to explore the resilience of teenagers who are working within and across all these stages every day. I wanted to show the struggle and beauty of one teen figuring out how to be and to become while she was hungry, while she was finding love and belonging, while she was discovering her path.

As an adult, I am still figuring out how to take care of myself and how to be a part of this complex world we live in. But what I do know is that I need others to help me. I am grateful for the people who love my family and grateful for the people who love me, who taught me how to love and be loved. This book would not exist without all of them.

CPSIA information can be obtained
at www.ICGtesting.com
Printed in the USA
LVOW11s2115020518
575705LV00004B/936/P